# NAVAJO TRIBAL BLOOD, REVENGE, AND BELIEFS

## Three Chile Charlie Adventures

7-23-23

Best of Luck & Best wishes
From Mom

*George Pinter*

This book is a work of fiction. Names, characters, businesses, organizations, places, events, and incidents either are the product of the author's imagination or are used fictitiously. Any resemblance to an actual person, living or dead, occurrences, or locals is coincidental.
The central character, Chile Charlie, is a fictional detective.

    All rights reserved. KDP, an Amazon, Inc. division, published Revenge in the United States. Library of Congress cataloging-in-publication data is on file with the Library of Congress.

First edition December 2021

Design Cover by a KDP

ISBN:9798389088474

Other books by George Pintar:

**FICTION:**

The Adventures of Chile Charlie
Fascinating New Mexico Stories
Musing of an Ostrich Farmer
A New Peek at Old West County
The Camel's Nose Maybe in the Tent
When is it Too Late?
Never Too Late
Navajo Traditional Spiritual Beliefs

**NONFICTION:**

Digging Deeper into Networking
Networking for Profit
The Fundamentals of Grant Writing
Building Stronger Communities

# ACKNOWLEDGMENT

Thanks to my family, colleagues, and editors for encouraging me to author this story. In my other books, you may have read about my fictitious character, Chile Charlie. He has become a pillar of strength in my life.

Thanks to the dozens of contributive thoughts, experiences, and research to do this book. Among the most helpful and supportive were Charmayne Samuelson, Bob Worthington, Heidi Anderson, Jon Samuelson, Janice Alexander, Efrem Carrasco, Maryann Costa, Austin Jones, and Lindsey Jones.

I want to thank my caregiver, Mary Holguin, who provided me with house cleaning and meal services while working on this book.

On a personal note, I thank my wife, Jean Natalie Pintar, for bearing with me during the writing phase of Chile Charlie's adventures; she always supported and encouraged me to write. Jean died before this book was published, but I know she would have given the book her seal of approval.

# NAVAJO TRIBAL BLOOD
# TABLE OF CONTENTS

PROLOGUE……………………………………….Page 1

Chapter One--*The Journey*……………………….Page 9

Chapter Two—*Land of Enchantment*…………Page 16

Chapter Three—*Bonding*………………………Page 26

Chapter Four—*Graystone*………………………Page 30

Chapter Five—*Magi Milly*………………………Page 40

Chapter Six—*Blue Notes*………………………Page 54

Chapter Seven—*Tribal Meeting*………………..Page 59

Chapter Eight—*First Day*………………………Page 63

Chapter Nine—*Second Day*……………………Page 74

Chapter Ten—*Third Day*………………………Page 85

Chapter Eleven—*Strange Friends*……………..Page 89

Chapter Twelve—*Evil Christmas Spirits*……Page 103

Chapter Thirteen — *Land of the People* ……… Page 107

Chapter Fourteen — *Perea Corrals* … … … … Page 111

Chapter Fifteen — *Braided Tail* … … … …….. Page 116

Chapter Sixteen — *Bad Day at Blackrock's* …. Page 127

Chapter Seventeen — *Black Heart* … ……...... Page 140

Chapter Eighteen — *Gift of the Spirits* … … …. Page 152

Chapter Nineteen — *Ceremony* … … … … …….. Page 159

# NAVAJO REVENGE

# TABLE OF CONTENTS

**CHAPTER ONE**
    *The Chapel* … … … … … … … … … … … Page 166

**CHAPTER TWO**
    *Strange behavior* … … … … … … … … … Page 170

**CHAPTER THREE**
    *Crimewave* … … … … … … … ……… … … Page 172

**CHAPTER FOUR**

*Zodiac Sign ... ... ... ... ... ... ... ... ... … ... Page 174*

**CHAPTER FIVE**

*The body ... ... ... ... ... ... ... …... ... ... ... Page 175*

**CHAPTER SIX**

*Discovery ... ... ... ... ... ... …... ... ... ... Page 178*

**CHAPTER SEVEN**

*A second body was found ... ... ... ... … .. Page 182*

**CHAPTER EIGHT**

*A hunch ... ... ... ... ... ... ... ... ... ... … ... Page 190*

**CHAPTER NINE**

*Early hostilities ... ... ... ... ... ... …... ... ... Page 192*

**CHAPTER TEN**

*The trip ... ... ... ... ... ... ... …... ... ... ... ... Page 198*

**CHAPTER ELEVEN**

*Finally, the arrival ... ... ... ... ... ... ... ... Page 206*

**CHAPTER TWELVE**

*One solution, new problem ... ... ... ... ... Page 228*

# NAVAJO TRADITIONAL SPIRITUAL BELIEFS

## TABLE OF CONTENTS

**CHAPTER ONE**

    Day One – Tohatch………………………． Page 232

**CHAPTER TWO**

    Day Two – Creation and Emergence…..． Page 254

**CHAPTER THREE**

    Day Three – Myths and Legends……..…． Page 266

**CHAPTER FOUR**

    Day Four–Myths & Legends Continued… Page 279

**CHAPTER FIVE**

    Day Four – Blue Rope……………………．Page 283

**CHAPTER SIX**

    Day Five – Salvation and Sin……．………．Page 295

**CHAPTER SEVEN**

**Recap……………………………….……...Page 305**

# ADVENTURE ONE

## TRIBAL BLOOD

### PROLOGUE

Jimmy Running Water and his childhood friend, Chris Leaping Bear, were of the Navajo Warm Springs Tribe near Gallup, New Mexico. It was late fall, and they sat under the shade of a fully grown Chinese elm tree and spoke with disgust of the poverty conditions of the reservation and the hardships they'd endured all their lives. They talked about what they wanted, primarily items of self-gratification like new clothes, money for entertainment, and a decent truck. Both Jimmy and Chris were twenty years of age and jobless. There weren't many good-paying jobs on the reservation that suited them, plus they lacked the skills and training for high-paying federal jobs. They were boys cast only for blue-collar jobs. Their only obstacle was laziness, and their only hope was crime.

Jimmy Running Water spent most of his teenage years engaged in misdemeanor crimes, mostly thefts from stores, unsuspecting tourists, family members, and, occasionally, livestock from local ranches. Chris Leaping Bear had always been Jimmy's lackey and complicit partner. Together, they had been arrested numerous times.

"Why did you ask me to meet you here," Leaping Bear asked Jimmy.

"I found a way to make enough money for us to get out of this godforsaken reservation," Running Water said.

"Like what? We can't go back into construction again. Everybody thinks we steal their tools. We're lucky they didn't call the cops last Time."

Running Water gave Chris a dismissive wave of his hand. "Eh, don't worry about it. *Tref* may be a Policeman, but he's my cousin, and you know what they say, 'Blood is thicker than whisky.'"

"Yeah, maybe, but I don't think Tref likes you. You better stick to the whisky."

Running Water smiled. "Greystone told me about a job and gave me the number of a man to call."

"Did you call him?"

"Yeah. The man told me about the black market for Indian relics and a storehouse full of valuable stuff at the Native American Museum in Gallup. He said there's a collection of Navajo ceremonial masks in the Inventory Room worth thousands of dollars," Jimmy said excitedly. "I want those masks. The question is, how do we get them? Any ideas?"

"No, you're always the one with the ideas," Chris replied.

Running Water thought for a moment. "Okay then. Please go to the museum and check out the layout, especially where the back door is and check out the security system and the night security guard's routine. Find out what times he checks the doors and how often. I wanna know everything."

"Okay. Sounds good to me."

"Meet me back here at one o'clock in three days. Then we'll come up with a plan then. I have other things I need to check out," Jimmy said.

The boys met again three days later under the same Chinese elm tree, which had lost half of its leaves by then.

"So, what did you find out?" Jimmy Running Water asked as he rubbed his hands to keep them warm.

"I discovered it would be hard to sneak into the museum. The security guard gets there at five p.m. and starts to make his rounds after all the employees leave. He checks all doors to ensure none have been left open by accident and rechecks them about every two hours during his entire shift. His desk is just inside and faces the front door," Leaping Bear reported. "I thought he might fall asleep, but the man stays awake all night. I don't think we can get in there undetected."

"We'll have to figure something out, then," Jimmy said.

"You mean we're still going to try to steal those masks anyhow?"

Jimmy gave his friend a grin with a sinister look. "Oh yes, we're going to get those masks for sure. It'll make a nice Christmas present."

Jimmy and Chris arrived at the front door of the Native American Museum at 8:15 p.m. that evening. They wore dark, hooded jackets and dirty, tattered clothes that made them look like vagrants, and each carried a small ceremonial drum. They sat with their backs to the front door and began beating their drums with a slow rhythmic sound that could barely be heard inside the museum. As time passed, the drums became louder and louder until the security guard finally got up from his chair, unlocked the front door, and stepped outside.

"You boys get . . ."

Before the guard completed his warning, Jimmy Running Water sprang up and grabbed him from behind in a tight bear hug. The guard struggled but was helpless against the powerful grip of his assailant. Chris Leaping Bear took a bottle of ether from his coat pocket and soaked a white handkerchief. He placed it tightly over the guard's mouth and nostrils. Jimmy turned his head to avoid a whiff of the ether. The guard fell limp in Jimmy's muscular arms within a few seconds.

They drugged the security guard inside and tied him upright in his chair with his head slumped down. The boys found their way to the Inventory Room and searched all the shelves filled with Native American relics. They rummaged throughout the room and the shelves until they found four ceremonial Kachina masks wrapped in red velvet cloths in a wooden case. Chris Leaping Bear pulled a large black cotton sack from inside his Jacket and placed the masks carefully in the bag. All was quiet, and the guard did not stir. The boys left through the back door, which locked automatically behind them.

Two hours after the break-in, Running Water and Leaping Bear arrived at the base of a canyon far north of the city. It was four weeks until Christmas, and the temperature hovered nearly thirty-two degrees. They pulled the hoods of their jackets tightly against their faces to keep warm.

"Get the shovels out of the truck, and let's find the hiding place for our treasure," Jimmy ordered. He had scouted the canyon a few days before and found a good spot to bury the sacred masks—

between a large piñon juniper tree and the canyon wall.

The desert looked different in the dark, but with flashlights, and considerable time, they found the spot. The digging began. Chris dug a four-foot square hole, four feet deep, while his friend held the flashlights. Jimmy placed the sack into the hole and carefully covered it with loose red earth to not pack it too tight.

"You think we'll be able to find this place two weeks from now," Chris asked.

Jimmy responded, "Yeah, I am sure I'll remember this place." He placed two nearby large, red sandstone rocks on the covered hole to mark the spot. He stepped back and admired his work. "It's going to be a good Christmas."

The two boys celebrated with whiskey and danced to the sound of their hand-held drums. Jimmy broke branches off a nearby tree and used them to smooth the ground over the freshly dug hole. They walked to their truck dragging the bushes behind them to conceal their footprints on the loose sand, then tied the bushes to the truck's bumper. They drove away, erasing any trace of their presence, and disappeared into the darkness.

▲▲▲▲▲

Dr. Lean Acothley, the Museum Director, arrived early the following morning and found his security guard bound to a chair. He called the Gallup Police Department immediately and inspected the entire museum for stolen items.

When the police arrived, the night security guard reported that he was overwhelmed by two vagrants wearing hooded jackets, and that was all he could remember. The police asked for a list of stolen items.

"Nothing of value has been taken," the Director replied.

# Chapter One

## *The Journey*

Chile Charlie was sound asleep when he felt movement on his mattress. Sir Gallagher, his seven-year-old fur-ball cat, had found his way onto Charlie's chest. His six a.m. ritual told his master it was time to face the new day. Charlie's eyes were still closed as he gave Sir Gallagher his morning back and belly rub.

"Thanks, Gallagher, you're a good alarm clock," he said with a raspy voice.

Sir Gallagher had done his duty. He jumped from the bed and waited for Charlie to do the same. It was a struggle. It took another fifteen minutes before his feet finally touched the floor. He followed his buddy to the kitchen, opened a can of kitty food, and pushed the start button on the coffee maker.

Chile Charlie lived in a condo on the second floor of a small complex. It was a modest home. His front door faced the city of Las Cruces, New Mexico. It led to a sitting room with two hallways, each leading to separate bedrooms. The kitchen in the back was sufficiently large for a single man. The back door in the kitchen opened to a concrete landing with stairs to the parking lot. Next to the kitchen was the living room with a glass sliding door that provided a panoramic view of the Organ Mountains and opened to a private patio. It was a comfortable home but lonely.

Charlie glanced out the rear sliding glass door to view the sunrise—another day. He sat in the living room staring at the mountains for almost an hour until the sun broke over the peaks. The sun shone brightly, with no clouds to clutter the view of the blue sky or morning fog to cover the majestic mountains' peaks.

God must have used his magical brush to paint this scene for me, Charlie thought, but it didn't bring a smile to his face, unlike before. Charlie hadn't smiled for some time. Gloom and melancholia had set in his heart. He sat on his leather chair for another hour before he got up to dress for his daily jog. He moved with sluggish motions as if lacking purpose.

A dirt hiking trail was less than fifty yards from his back door, and every morning, come rain or shine, Charlie took his five-foot, eleven-inch frame for a two-mile run. He enjoyed running the picturesque narrow canyons and rocky arroyo trails and watching the desert's wildlife. Lately, it has been his only tranquility from his burden.

The first mile started with a slow military jog, then a faster jog, and finally, an entire run for the last quarter of a mile. He returned an hour later. The final fifty yards of his run were slightly uphill, which gave his cardiovascular system a good workout.

Although Chile Charlie was in good physical condition for a forty-eight-year-old man, he breathed heavily, exhausted from his run. He bent over and placed his hands on his knees to regain normal breathing, but he still had stairs to climb. Determinately, he ran up the stairs, two steps at a time, until he reached the top landing to the kitchen door.

Charlie stepped inside and slumped down onto a chair nearest the patio sliding door. When he heard a banging at the kitchen door, Charlie hadn't caught his breath. It was his neighbor, Bob, who lived in the condo below. They had become friends when Charlie first moved in eighteen months ago.

Bob was in his early forties and had a physic of a couch potato—not much exercise. Bob motioned that he wanted in, and Charlie reluctantly forced himself to get up and unlock the door.

"Why am I blessed with your presence this morning, Bob," Charlie asked.

Bob said, "Wait, let me catch my breath first. Those stairs are killers. No matter how slowly I climb them, I always need time to regain my breath. I'm sure the 3,900-foot elevation has something to do with it."

"Bob, you'd suffocate if you lived in Colorado. The elevation is a mile high there." Charlie gave Bob a grin as if to say, find a better excuse for being out of shape.

The tone in Charlie's voice did not go unnoticed. Bob helped himself to a glass of water and drank it in large gulps. "I came up here to check on you, to see how you're doing. I noticed you haven't been yourself for some time now."

"Thanks, but I don't need any looking after."

"It's been quiet up here. My wife and I don't hear the Randy Granger, Carlos Nakai, or any other Native American music that you used to play all the time. We kind of like that music."

"The CDs are on top of the stereo. Take them if you miss them so much," Charlie said almost angrily.

"You never talked like that to me before, Charlie. This is not you. What's going on with you?"

Charlie realized he had hurt his friend's feelings. "I'm sorry, Bob. You're right. I'm just going through some things right now."

"What kind of things?"

"Nothing I care to discuss?"

"Nothing you care to discuss. Do you know whom you're talking to? I'm a psychologist, remember? And more than that, I'm your friend. I can help you work through whatever's weighing on your mind."

Charlie inhaled deeply, held the air briefly, and released it. "Too many things have gone wrong in my life, Bob—my divorce from my high school sweetheart. After sixteen years of marriage, I lost my wife, four children, and home. It was my fault, though."

"You never told me about that, Charlie."

"It's too painful to talk about. But there's more to it. I later met this wonderful woman, and we were married for six years . . . she died three years ago. Cancer took her away from me," he said with quivering lips and down-casted eyes. "I started drinking heavily and pretty much lost everything. I only had my tractor, so I moved here to escape all those memories."

"Wow. I didn't know that." Bob was disappointed that he didn't know his friend as well as he thought.

"It doesn't matter where you move," Charlie said, "the memories always follow you and sometimes haunt you. It hit me suddenly and has eaten at me for a long time."

"You know, Charlie. Words can't fix a man. They can only direct him. And you can't go around searching for answers. Sometimes the answers will find you. But you must have an open mind and an open heart." Bob looked about the room. He saw the stack of Native American music on the entertainment shelf.

"You know, there's a reason this place is called the Land of Enchantment, and there's a reason you ended down here. Maybe you should travel up north and find a priest from one of those old missions to guide you, or perhaps . . . some Indian shaman on the reservations."

The room was silent for a few minutes.

"You know Bob, for a psychologist, you sure give strange advice, but maybe that's what I need, some odd in my life.

## Chapter Two

*Land of Enchantment*

Charlie spent most of the morning having his 1959 El Camino serviced for his journey. The afternoon was spent at the Mesilla Mall buying new clothes and a giant suitcase to put them in. It was almost 4:00 p.m. when his car was packed and ready to go. Charlie placed his dark earth military backpack on the passenger seat. He stepped back to admire his car, a newly painted 1959 El Camino, a cream color with a turquoise stripe from front to back. The colors of the earth, he thought.

Charlie honked his horn twice, and Bob came out of his condo holding and petting Sir Gallagher.

"I see you're all ready to go. Where are you headed?" Bob said.

"I think I'll head up to Gallup first, then who knows?

"Stay at the El Rancho Hotel. I hear it's quite famous."

"I'll keep that in mind. Take good care of my buddy and keep an eye on my place, will you? And . . . thank you, Bob."

"No problem. But can I ask you a question?"

"Sure. You can ask me anything, friend."

"I know it's none of my business, but I wondered. You said you lost everything except your tractor. You don't have a job. So how is it that you can afford a nice condo?"

Charlie smiled at Bob's curious nature. "My mother died a few years back, and shortly after I moved here, my father passed away too. He left the farm to me, but I wasn't about to return to farming, and I sold it."
"It must have been a large farm," Bob said jokingly.

"It was substantial."

The long drive made Charlie feel relaxed. He loved the desert of southern New Mexico, and the scenery eased his mind. Charlie had read a lot about the history of the state. He looked at the landscape with amazement, the same land on which the Spanish Conquistadors once rode their horses—the *Jornada Del Muerto,* Journey of the Dead. He thought of the Native Americans, the Apache, the Hopi, the Zuni, and the Navajo, the people who were once rulers of this land. He inserted a CD into the player and listened to his Native American flute music—the perfect music for this journey.

Exhausted, he drove into the well-lit parking lot of the Hotel El Rancho at 9:30 p.m. He hoped there would be a room available. He should have made a room reservation before leaving Las Cruces. Charlie counted the number of vehicles in the parking lot. Fortunately, there weren't too many.

He could hardly keep his eyes open as he strolled into the lobby, where a half-asleep Front Desk clerk stood behind the counter.

"Do you have a single room available on the ground floor? I plan to stay in Gallup for several weeks." Charlie said.

Charlie was assigned to the first floor, room 113. He entered and immediately set the thermostat at sixty-five degrees, the best temperature for sleeping. He went directly to bed and dozed off within seconds. He woke up with a start when he heard an unusual noise. It took a few seconds before he realized he was in a hotel room and not in his bed at home. Must be a hotel guest out in the hallway, he thought. He closed his eyes and was almost asleep when he heard a loud knock on his door. He opened his eyes but didn't move. Am I dreaming, he thought. Then another loud knock at the door. This was no dream. He jumped out of bed, wearing an olive drab t-shirt and black sweatpants, and opened the door. It was a lady in a short lavender, almost transparent, teddy nightgown that left little to the imagination.

"Help me," she pled. "A man just broke into my room and asked for money." Her cries and the pounding on the door alerted other guests. The hallway quickly filled up with curious on-lookers.

"Is he still in your room?" Charlie asked.

"No, he just ran out and down the hallway!"
"Wait here!" Charlie rushed to his bed, grabbed a Beretta .380 caliber pistol he kept under his pillow, and rushed out into the hallway.

"Which room?" he asked the strange woman.

She pointed down the hall. "There, the room with the opened door!"

Charlie stood next to the door. It was slightly opened. He pushed it and quickly glanced inside — nothing. He stepped into the room slowly and cautiously, eyes scanning back and forth from right to left, holding the gun tightly against his right hip. He checked the bathroom, the closet, and under the bed, but no one was there. The room was clear of intruders. He started for the door but stopped abruptly when he saw a crumpled blue paper on the floor by the door. He hadn't noticed it before, but he wasn't looking for trash — he was searching for a person.

As Charlie picked up the envelope, he heard someone whistle outside followed. Then there was the discordant roar of a car, which sounded like it needed a tune-up, followed by the screeching of tires. He looked out the window and saw no movement in the parking lot. Chile Charlie placed the crumbled paper in the pocket of his sweatpants and returned to the hallway where the strange woman was still waiting by his door. Only a handful of curious people were left in the hallway, primarily men gawking at the woman in the lavender teddy. Charlie rushed her into his room but kept the door open.

"There was no one in your room," he said. He called the Gallup Police Department and reported the attempted robbery. The dispatcher informed him that an officer would arrive soon.

"I'm Charlie, by the way," he said to the woman. "But everyone calls me Chile Charlie. You better stay here until the police arrive. They'll want to dust your room for fingerprints, don't want to contaminate it."

"My name is Dolly, Dolly Thompson," she said with a tremor. Her lips and chin trembled.

"Are you okay?"

"Just a bit shaken up, I guess.

Charlie glanced at her nightgown, which did not give her body much protection from the sixty-five-degree room temperature in the room, or modesty for that matter—it revealed her mature figure. Dolly became aware of her nightgown and crossed her arms in front of her with embarrassment.

"Oh, I'm sorry," Charlie said. He realized he had been staring at her body and was embarrassed. He quickly took the top blanket from his bed and placed it on Dolly's back for her to wrap around her body. There was an awkward silence for a moment.

"I was so frightened that I didn't realize I wasn't properly dressed," Dolly explained.

Charlie thought to relieve her of the embarrassment and trauma with detached conversation. He had detected a distinct Chicago nasal resonance in Dolly. "You sound like you're from Chicago."

"Why, yes," she said surprisingly.

"So, what brings you to the Land of Enchantment?"
"I'm a professor of Anthropology at Loyola University Chicago. I'm on a sabbatical to research Navajo spiritual traditions for my book. I plan to venture out in the four corners area for a few months."

"Are you Navajo?"

Dolly chuckled. It was Charlie's first honest look at her. She stood straight and seemed to have a glimpse of propriety about her. She had beautiful straight white teeth, brown eyes, straight dark brown hair, and an aura of innocence on that forty-something face. He had already gotten a good look at her curvy, mature, and voluptuous body, but the combination of her smile, voice, and innocence made Charlie want to hug this strange woman. She was attractive, and she was black.

"No, of course, I'm not Navajo," Dolly giggled.

Twenty-five minutes later, Officer Red Shoe arrived at Charlie's room. He listened carefully and took notes as Dolly Thompson slowly reported the incident. The officer's questions conjured up the incident in her mind, and her body began to quiver, her lips trembled, and tears flowed. She was still traumatized by the stranger's abrupt entrance into her room. Her words came slowly.

"I showered around 8:15, jumped into bed, and quickly fell asleep. Then, there was a loud knock on the door. I asked, 'Who's there?' The man answered,

'Hotel Security, please open the door.'" Dolly continued. "As I opened the door, he rushed in, pushed me back, and demanded I give him money. I said 'No,' gave him a hard push, and rushed to Charlie's door for help. That's when the man ran down the hall."

"Can you describe the intruder," Officer Red Shoe asked?

"He was around Charlie's height . . ."

"I'm almost six feet tall," Charlie said abruptly.
Dolly continued. "He had long black hair with a long braided ponytail that dangled below his shoulders from the right side of his head. He appeared to be Native American."

"Can you remember what he was wearing, ma'am?" the officer asked.

"He had a red and black plaid shirt, and when he ran down the hallway, I noticed he had blue jeans and reddish-brown work-type boots." Dolly paused. "That's all I can remember."

"Thank you. We'll have a unit patrolling the area tonight," Officer Red Shoe said. In the meantime, I'm going to your room to dust the door knobs for possible fingerprints, but it doesn't sound like he was there long enough to leave any evidence."

"Wait! I just remembered," Dolly exclaimed. "When I pushed him, I noticed a small scar on the left side of his face, like a knife cut him."

Officer Red Shoe smiled. "Ma'am, around here, many men have scars like that on their faces."

Dolly and Charlie were left alone in his room. They faced each other as they attempted to gauge the other's thoughts.

"Thank you, Charlie." She smiled at him. "I think the café is still open. Maybe I can buy you a cup of coffee."

Charlie needed to be more eager. He was still tired from his trip. "How about we meet for breakfast at the hotel restaurant instead?"

Dolly accepted his invitation.

## Chapter Three

## *Bonding*

Chile Charlie had a spring in his step the following morning as he headed to the restaurant. He admired the lobby with its highly polished mahogany stairs that led to the second floor and the numerous autographed pictures of various Hollywood celebrities displayed on the walls, like John Wayne, Marilyn Monroe, Clark Gable, and the like.

Charlie arrived at the café before Dolly. The walls were also plastered with pictures of notable politicians, tycoons, and Hollywood celebrities who had stayed at the hotel and eaten at the restaurant. The tables were covered with traditional red and white-checkered linen, and the legs were in tall cowboy boots, an unusual but nice touch. He ordered black coffee and checked the menu for *huevos rancheros*.

Dolly arrived. Charlie stood up and pulled a chair out for her. They sat across from each other.
He thought she looked much different than she did last night, more stunning.

She smiled. "Did you sleep well," she asked. "Like a log."

Dolly ordered black coffee and studied the menu. "What are you having?"

"I am having their *huevos rancheros*." Charlie answered.

"Too spicy for me," she said. "I'm having pancakes with a sunny-side-up egg." Then, there was an awkward silence, and they looked at one another as if this was their first meeting. She thought Charlie looked different than she remembered—clean-shaven, hair combed, black jeans, a neatly pressed tan cotton shirt, and brown leather suspenders. Nice, she thought. "Tell me about you, Charlie."

"Well, I was born in St. David, Illinois. It was a small coal-mining town comprised of nine hundred people of three ethnic groups—the English, the Italians, and the Croatians. I attended school there. I was good at sports and later received a scholarship to Bradley University, where I played football, Baseball, and ran track. After two years of college, I joined the Army, and when I got out, I decided the best thing to do was to finish school. I got my master's degree in education from Western Illinois University, and I ended up teaching high school and, later, 7th and 8th grades.

"During the summers, I helped my father on the family farm. I'm divorced, widowed, and have four kids . . . had four kids, but that's a different story." Charlie studied her face. "What's your story, Dolly?"

"I grew up in the Cabrini Green Housing Projects in the north part of Chicago during the 60s and 70s. My mother was from rural Mississippi, worked the cotton fields, and at thirteen, she was married off to the town drunk, my father. They moved to Chicago in 1966, and two years later, I was born Dolly Sweet Thompson. I learned quickly about the hood, the murder, and the mayhem there. I was eleven when I saw my first dead body. But I was one of the lucky ones. I graduated from high school and then studied Archaeology at Loyola University, emphasizing Native American Studies. And that's why I'm here."

Their meals arrived, and Charlie and Dolly continued with small talk. They finished their breakfast with additional cups of coffee and more small talk.

"Dolly, would you like to go sightseeing with me today? Gallup is known for its wonderful parks, wall paintings, and museums."

"Sure. Give me a few minutes to freshen up. I'd like to see Gallup in the light of day."

"Just knock on my door when you're ready. You know where I live," Charlie bantered.

## Chapter Four

*Greystone*

Nate Greystone woke up to the coldness of the morning and the sound of barking dogs. He had slept in one of the back rooms of the gambling house and immediately remembered the deep trouble he was in. He had been in Gallup for three days, away from the ranch, gambling away all his money. Though usually a good gambler, his luck could have been better lately. Nate always made money with his schemes, which generally involved a crime. The police interrogated him numerous times for different crimes, but they could never pin anything on him, not even for complicity.

He grew up as a mischievous and troubled boy in the remote desert of Teec Nos Pos, Arizona. By the age of thirteen, he had been involved in one kind of trouble or another—fights, thefts, shoplifting, and constant truancy. His parents thought the evil spirits lived in him and called the *haatalii*, the medicine man, to perform the exorcism ritual to expel those spirits, but the evil spirits were too strong. The elders spoke with his parents. They did not want evil spirits in their community. Jimmy was sent to live with his grandparents in a far removed place near Navajo, New Mexico.

Jimmy had been staying at Blackrock's, a small, remote ranch house hidden among the hills seven miles south of Gallup. It was popular with the local criminal element and known for its gambling, drinking, drugs, prostitution, and sanctuary for young female runaways. Jimmy wasn't a drinker or a drug user, but he enjoyed gambling and the company of the women and other misfits.

He got up and walked towards the body of a man sleeping on the floor, near his cot, with a coat draped over him like a blanket. Nate shook the man with his foot. He knew this was the safest way to wake this man. Otherwise, he may end up with a knife to his gut.

"Come on. Get up," Nate said.

The body didn't move. Nate shoved harder with his foot. "Come on, Waste Water, get up. I must go. I need a ride."

The man moaned, turned away from Nate, and pulled his coat over his head.

"I have some information for you if you want to make money."

The man shifted into a fetal position under the coat. "Go away, leave me alone. I'm too tired, and you live too far," the man said with a groggy voice.

"Is ten thousand dollars not enough for a ride to my house?" Nate Greystone asked.

The man pushed the coat away and sprang up to a sitting position. "What are you talking about?"

"I'll tell you, Running Water, but first, take me home."

▲▲▲▲▲

Charlie and Dolly stopped at the desolate intersection of Defiance Draw Road and County Road 1 to figure out where they were and how to get to the *Tsayatoh* Government Chapter Office. They had spent three hours in the morning casually touring several sights in Gallup — the Railroad, the Navajo Totem, the wall paintings in the business district that depicted the city's historical development, and the Native American Museum.

It was still early in the day, and Dolly wanted to visit the Navajo Chapter near Defiance. Charlie had decided to take his El Camino via the scenic route north through the village of Mentmore and then west on County Road 1. They zigzagged in several directions throughout the sage-covered country with a sparse population of piñon trees until they arrived at the intersection.

"Charlie, are we lost?" Dolly asked.

"Nope. We're not lost. I'm confused and can't get GPS on my cell phone. Service is hit and misses around here."

The driver's door was suddenly opened, and before Charlie could react, he felt the cold edge of a knife pressed against his throat. They had not seen the figure hidden in the shade of a piñon tree near the intersection.

"Lady, get out of the car and keep your hands up, and don't try anything, or you'll become a widow." The man said.

Dolly immediately exited the car, frightened, with her hands halfway up. Not again, she thought.

The assailant pressed the broad side of the blade up against the chin, forcing Charlie to tilt his head back.

"And you, white man. Come out very slowly. I don't want to hurt anybody; I want your car." He reached in and grabbed a handful of Charlie's hair with the right hand while he pressed the knife against the throat with the other. He yanked Charlie out of the car and discovered he was a tall white man. "Get down on your knees!" he ordered, pressing Charlie's head down.

"Please don't hurt him!" Dolly shouted.

The assailant turned to Dolly. "Shut up, lady, and back away from the car!"

Charlie felt the blade ease against his throat. He raised his left hand, pushed the assailant's hand away, grabbed the knife hand simultaneously with his right hand, and sprung up against the assailant with the quickness of a rattlesnake. Charlie spun the man around but lost his grip. The man slashed at

Charlie, cut his left forearm, and turned to run. He took two steps and stopped abruptly as he faced the dark, ominous barrel of a handgun.

"Don't make me shoot you. Dolly shouted. "It won't be the first time I've killed a man! Her eyes were wide and wild, and her heart pounded hard against her chest.

The assailant turned again to run, only to meet the full force of Charlie's fist. The man went down and dropped the knife. Charlie looked at the Bowie knife with a bone handle and a wide fourteen-inch blade; he picked up the knife, placed the weight of his left knee on the man's chest, and pressed the blade against his throat. "How does it feel to be on the edge of death?"

"Don't kill me! Please don't! I wasn't going to hurt anybody. I just needed the car," the assailant pled.

Charlie studied the man's face. He noticed the smooth dark skin and the frightened brown eyes. This was no man. This was just a boy. He yanked the boy up by the shirt collar and slammed him against the car with the forearm of the hand holding the Bowie knife. He wore a heavy, tan, black, wool plaid shirt under a black hoodie and an olive-drab wool coat over the hoodie.

"What's the matter with you, boy? You got mush for brains? You slashed at me, cut me, and you almost got yourself killed!"

Chile Charlie noticed Dolly still had the gun pointed at the boy. He nodded for her to point the gun down.

He shook the boy. "All this just for a joy ride?" Charlie was furious. His new shirt sleeve was cut and moist with blood.

"It wasn't for a joy ride," the boy said. "I just needed the car."

"What was the big hurry?"

"I need to get home to my grandmother. She's alone, and I haven't been home for a few days to help her at the ranch." He felt like a loser; he dishonored the authentic way of Navajo. He had never committed a serious crime like this before. He was supposed to be the smart one. This wasn't how his grandparents raised him.

"All you had to do was ask for a ride." Charlie released the boy. "We'll take you home."

"It's too far, about thirty miles from here up by Crystal, east of Navajo."

"That's all right." Charlie hands him his handkerchief to wipe the blood from his nose. "What's your name, boy?"

"Nate Greystone. Everyone calls me Greystone."

"Well, Nate, do you have a sheath for this sword?"

Greystone kept his knife in an old brown leather sheath with leather sewn edges, fringes, and beadwork of turquoise, red, black, and white in the image of a Kachina's face. He reached under his opened shirt and pulled out the sheath from the inside of his belt at the small of his back.

Charlie was impressed with the leatherwork. "This is fancy leather and beadwork. Looks like something out of *Dances with Wolves*. He inserted the knife into the sheath. "Go ahead and get in the car," Charlie ordered.

"Are you going to call the police," Greystone asked?

"Only if I can get cell service, or you try something stupid again."

The boy wasn't sure what Charlie meant, but he got into the car on the passenger side.

"And don't touch anything," Charlie commanded. He walked to the back of his El Camino and motioned Dolly to join him.

"Dolly, are you all right?" He didn't wait for an answer. "I didn't know you were packing a gun."

"It's not mine. It's yours," Dolly said, "I saw you put it in the glove box this morning."

Chile, Charlie had to ask. "Did you kill a man once?"

"No. I was scared and didn't know what else to say," Dolly said. She smiled. "But then, the day's still young."

Chile Charlie nodded with approval. "Thank God for the hood. Let's get out of here."
The drive was silent. Dolly sat between Charlie and Nate Greystone. She felt the warmth of Charlie's body. Nice, she thought.

Charlie drove, deep in thought. I was carjacked in broad daylight by a young Navajo punk kid in the middle of nowhere. I'm traveling with a black woman, who I just met last night and was the victim of an attempted robbery and who almost killed this punk kid. And this is only my second day here. What did I get myself into? What's next?

## Chapter Five

### *Magi Milly*

Magi Milly sat on a faded red, wooden rocking chair in front of her hogan, a traditional Navajo octagonal homemade pine logs with a conical roof of mud and timber. She was a small, bony woman with a prominent chin and deep crevices on her face caused by days in the sun and age. Her gray hair was pulled back into a folded ponytail and kept behind her head with a thin leather ribbon. She wore a faded burgundy Navajo shirt and a long sleeve velvet blouse that hung loosely on her thin body. She also wore a narrow silver bracelet and a necklace of squash blossom and turquoise. An old horse blanket draped her chair to protect her from the hardwood.

For the *Dine*—the Navajo people—the front doors always face east, so the first thing to see in the mornings was the "Father Sun." For Milly, which didn't matter. She sat outside her home every morning before the light rose to the east and waited for the sun to awaken the desert. Milly watched it until it was about two fingers above the horizon, then her day began.

Milly tended to her livestock—two horses, four cattle, and a large flock of sheep—every morning when her grandson wasn't home to help. After breakfast, she returns to her rocking chair to meditate and chant her songs until the sun becomes unbearable or something unexpected interrupts her mornings.

♦♦♦♦♦♦♦♦♦

Charlie gazed across the landscape of red desert covered with sage and pinon trees and, farther on the horizon, to the red sandstone hills and the pine-covered slopes of the *Lukachukai* Mountains. He was astounded by the vast emptiness before him. How does one survive out here? The silliness of his question struck him. These are the Navajo people. They survived long before the white Europeans stepped foot in this country.

"So, Nate, what were you doing out here in the middle of nowhere," Charlie asked.

"I was walking home. My friend gave me a ride from Gallup, but he didn't have enough gas to take me home, so he dropped me off at the freeway, and I walked. I was resting under that tree when you showed up."

"Do you do many carjackings?" Dolly said.

"No, that was my first time," Greystone responded in a low voice, ashamed of his behavior.

His response made Dolly more curious. "Why'd you do it?"

"I needed to get home. We have a sheep ranch, and I've been gone for a while. I left my grandmother alone for three days. She has had no one else to help her since her grandfather died. She's ancient. I guess I got scared."

His story did not move Charlie. "You're scared of an old woman? How old is she?" he asked.

"She's ninety-three."

Chile Charlie shook his head. He's afraid of an old lady, but he's brave enough to carjack us and fight me, he thought. He chuckled. "A young brave afraid of a ninety-three-year-old woman."

"You don't know my grandmother," he growled.

Greystone directed Charlie onto a dirt road and traveled for several more miles. "I see my Hogan," Greystone said as he pointed in the direction.

"A hogan?" Charlie said, surprised. "I've never seen a real hogan." He looked hard but only saw two stunted Juniper trees in the distance.

Dolly could not see it either. "Are you sure, Greystone," Dolly asked.

"Just follow the road," Greystone said.

Chile Charlie was curious to see a Navajo hogan. He was aware that hogan meant *earth home* in the *Dine* language. He had seen them in movies and pictures in history class, but this was the first time he had visited one.

They arrived. An authentic Hogan with smoke billowing through a stack stood on a hill in the flat valley. It was surrounded by corrals, a stable with horses, an outhouse, and an old rusting 1970 Ford truck. It was like one of those pictures he had seen on *Arizona Highways* and in *New Mexico* magazine.

Milly sat rocking in her chair outside next to the east door when the El Camino arrived. She looked uncomfortable and bewildered at seeing her grandson with an uninvited guest.

Nate quickly got out of the car. He was happy to see his grandmother, but she did not look happy. Though Greystone was twenty, she still worried about him. She had raised him in the traditional ways of the Navajo to maintain a *Balance of Life*, even if there was a wrong, and with her grandson, there was always evil.

"Young Owl, where have you been? Why were you gone so long? I needed your help." A frown appeared on her dark, weather-beaten face. "You should not be gone for so long."

"But, Grandma, it was only three days. I was in Gallup, and I couldn't get a ride back home," he explained with his eyes cast to the gown.
"Yes, but the sheep needed to be tended. That's how we survive, and I have no one else to help. You know that."

"I'm sorry, Grandmother," he said with contrition.

Charlie and Dolly watched the chastisement. They slowly exited the car with embarrassed smiles.

The old woman remained stoic and eyed them for a moment. A tall white man and a black woman, this is a sign, she thought. She turned her eyes to the desert and scanned the sky, then the land. "Look," she said to the strangers as she pointed to several dust funnels moving about in the desert. "Devils dancing in the wind. You never know what the spirits will bring next," she said.

"My name is Charlie, and this is Dolly." He didn't know what to make of this older woman, but he spoke reverently.

"I am Magi Milly. Why does my grandson have blood on his face, and why have you bled from your arm?"

"It was a misunderstanding," Charlie said. He removes the sheath with the Bowie knife from his belt and hands it to the old woman. "This belongs to your grandson."

Milly takes the knife and stares at it. "This was a gift to Young Owl from his grandfather. His great-grandfather made it." She turns to her grandson.

"Young Owl, go tend to the horses," she commanded.

Milly walked directly to the door and motioned Charlie and Dolly to join her. She walked with a four-foot staff of mesquite wood with leather wrapping adorned with turquoise beads, two silver jingle bells, and two hawk feathers.

The structures haven't changed much from earlier times, Dolly thought. She guessed the hogan was about twenty-five feet in diameter. She also took note of the construction—the eight-inch diameter post at each point of the octagon, the chinking in the gaps between the pine logs, and the pole rafters that make up the conical roof. She wanted to take pictures for her book but thought not to offend.

Charlie was impressed and in awe of Milly's home. An old flat-top iron stove with wood burning and crackling in the firebox sat at the west end, vented with a stovepipe that rose through the roof.

There were no pictures on the wall, just paintings, a dry sheepskin, dreamcatchers, and Indian blankets hung on several wood racks. There were two twin beds, one on the north side and the other on the south. Lever action .30-.30 caliber rifles hung on single gun racks on the wall above the beds. A dresser and a nightstand stood on the side of each bed, and along the southeastern wall was a worn-out, burgundy leather couch with a mesquite wood coffee table in front. Carpets of earth-tone colors covered the aged and squeaky wood floor planks.

Charlie noticed the wood shelves with several sticks of cut sage and jars filled with what appeared to be herbs or spices—he wasn't sure.

They sat on a willow log bench and table in the middle of the house. Magi Milly poured coffee and sat across from the strange guest. She reached into her pock, removed a smoking pipe, and struck a match against her leather belt to light it. She breathed in and exhaled the smoke from her nostrils and sat relaxed. "Thank you for bringing Young Owl home. It is important to have him here."

"Why do you call him 'Young Owl'? I thought his name was Nate," Charlie said.

Milly looked out the window on the north side, where she could see Young Owl curry combing one of the horses. "He is wise but too young to know it, she explained. "It is the war name given when young. It's the only name that counts and is kept secret within the family. The name is only used in one's *Blessing Way Ceremony* or when a Singer performs a cure." Milly puffed on her pipe. "Young Owl visits too often with the black hearts," she said as she continued to look out the window. She turned and noticed the confused looks of her guest.

"Other boys whose hearts are black and evil," Milly explained. "I see the good spirit in Young Owl, but I have not been able to make it appear. When he was sent to me by his parents, I gave him a medicine bag to always carry with him. I hoped it would keep his evil spirits away." She glances out the window again. "He keeps it hidden inside his pants as if he were ashamed of his Navajo heritage."

Milly surprised Chile Charlie. For an old woman, she was well-spoken and spry, not feeble, nor spoke with an old gruff voice.

"Well, Magi Milly, don't worry. We're not calling the police on Young Owl. I'm sure he's a good kid and doesn't need more problems."

Jimmy walked into the house and poured himself a cup of coffee. "It's cold outside," he announced.

"Young Owl, you need to thank our guest and apologize. They are not calling the Tribal Police."

"Thank you, Mr. Charlie . . ."

"Charlie. Everyone calls me Chile Charlie, but you can call me Charlie."

"Thank you, Charlie and Dolly. I'm sorry for my bad behavior. I will pay the hospital bill for your cut and buy you a new shirt."

"Don't worry about it. It's just a scratch, and this is an old shirt anyway."

"Is Chile Charlie your war name," Milly asked.

"Grandma, white men don't get war names," Greystone interrupted, "but Chile Charlie does sound good."

Everyone laughed except Milly. "Mr. Charlie, I can see your good spirit but troubles in your eyes."

"It's probably from the wind and sand," he said jokingly to conceal his embarrassment.

"Your eyes speak, and I hear them," Milly told him.

Charlie didn't know how to respond. This is a strange woman. We need to go, he thought. He averted his eyes towards Dolly and then back to Milly. "I think it's time for us to go. We've intruded enough . . ."

"Listen to her, Mr. Charlie," Nate blurted out, "she may be an old woman, but she is very wise. She knows things."

"Well, it's getting late, and we need to get to the *Tsayatoh* office before they close," Charlie said.

"Yes, I'm a professor from a university in Chicago, and I'm doing comparative research on tribal rituals," Dolly said. I hope to get information and some leads from the tribal chapters." She explained her reason for coming to New Mexico and shared the incident at the El Rancho Hotel. When she gave them the description of the suspect, Milly and Nate made subtle glances at each other.

"Charlie, where are you from," Milly asked.

"I live in Las Cruces now." He explained how he arrived in the land of Enchantment.

"Why are you here, in the reservations?" Milly asked.

"I just thought I'd get to know the country better and clear my head," Charlie said.

"Clear your head from your trouble? That's why you come to see Magi Milly," she stated.

"No. I was told to find a priest from one of the old missions or a shaman from the reservation to help me with some mystical therapy. Do you know where I can find one? He chuckled to make light of the conversation.

"Grandmother knows of many Shamans," Nate Greystone said.

"Your grandmother knows Shaman?" Chile Charlie asked surprisingly.

Greystone looked at his grandmother, then back at Charlie. "She is Shaman."

Milly inhaled deeply from her pipe. She held the smoke momentarily, then blew it upwards slowly until her lungs were empty. Milly concentrated intently on the smoke as if she saw something in it. She glanced directly at Charlie with her dark brown eyes. "Chile Charlie, come with me."

Milly signaled Greystone with her eyes to stay with Dolly, then walked out the door. Charlie curiously obeyed and followed her outside to the edge of an overlook behind the hogan.

Scanning the open land and the red cliffs on the southern horizon, Milly pointed to the desert with her staff. "Everything that makes the people comes from Mother Earth. People must find balance by becoming one with her." Milly said.

"So, it's the Navajo Middle Way Balance I Need to find?" Charlie asked.

"You need to purify your body and cleanse the bad spirit from your mind. Then, you must learn to become one with Mother Earth."

"How do I purify myself and become one with the earth," He asked.

"I will prepare the ceremony for you. Come back in three days. Bring only the clothes you wear and a blanket. When the healing occurs, you will be alone for three days with Mother Earth. You will get to know her."

## Chapter Six

*Blue Notes*

Greystone rode horseback as he escorted Charlie and Dolly to Indian Service Route 12, the main road that would take them back to Interstate 40. It was past 4:00 p.m. and too late to stop at the *Tsayatoh* Chapter Office. It was closed.

Chile Charlie and Dolly were back at the restaurant of the El Rancho Hotel by early evening. Dolly had a glass of cabernet wine, and Charlie had a prickly pear margarita.

"Did you notice how Milly and Greystone looked at each other when I mentioned the robber's description," Dolly asked?

"I did, and that reminds me, I found a blue crumpled-up note on the floor in your room last night. I forgot to give it to you."

"It's not mine," Dolly said. "What did it say?"

"I don't know. I thought it was yours, and I wasn't about to pry. It's in the pocket of my sweatpants."

Dolly and Charlie stared at one another. "The robber!" they said collectively.

"He must've dropped it when I shoved him!" Dolly exclaimed.

"Shhh, don't want the whole world to know," Charlie warned.

They downed their drinks and walked briskly to Charlie's room.

Charlie went to the closet where he had left sweatpants in his large suitcase. He took the note out of his pocket. They both sat on the edge of the bed as Charlie unfolded the note. It was a light blue, four-inch square, a ruled paper that looked like it had been ripped from a notepad. Dolly leaned into Charlie, almost cheek to cheek, to read the note. It was scribbled in black ink.

*waste water house Tohatchi tomorrow 7pm see li*

"What do you make of it, Charlie?

"Whoever wrote this note can't spell or punctuate. Looks like he was in a hurry, not sure, though." He studied the note further. "Waste water . . ." he pauses to think. "He must be a plumber, or he works on septic systems. Waste water is also called grey water, which means it's an RV or a mobile home."

"It says house."

"For some people, an RV is a house."

"We need to give this note to the police," Dolly suggested.

"We don't have time for that. It's 6:40 now. That means the robber is on his way to Tohatchi right now. Can you identify him if we see him?"

"I'm sure I can. Let's go!" Dolly said. "Wow, this is like the movies."

They arrived in Tohatchi at 7:12 p.m. and began their search at the north side of the town by the high school.

"What are we looking for, Charlie," Dolly asked.

"People working outside on a septic system or anyone walking around outside. I want to find the man who tried to rob you."

They saw no signs of human activity, and the suspect would have been difficult to recognize if there were any. The town was dark, except for a few dim street lights, and the lights turned on inside houses with closed shades. Chile Charlie drove back onto Highway 491 and headed to the south part of the town, which was even darker than the north side. They drove on the paved road past several houses and the *Tohatchi* Chapter building until they came to a Y-intersection. To the right was a dark cul-de-sac, and to the left was a dirt road with a few houses. Charlie turned left. They were several yards up the road when the front end of the El Camino began to shake. Charlie stopped to check.

"Well, our adventure is over. I got a flat tire on the front left side."

"You need some help?"

"No, but you can keep me company. Don't worry about snakes out here. It's too cold for them. You won't see them till spring."

Just then, Charlie heard an engine roar and an even louder bang that echoed throughout the small community.

"Is someone shooting," Dolly asked with concern. She had grown up where loud bangs were heard almost nightly, a signal that usually meant someone was injured or killed.

"No, that sounded like a backfire from a car. I guess people around here have something against car tune-ups. It sounded like they were in some hurry too." Then, it struck him. "Damn! That might've been our boy."

## Chapter Seven

*Tribal Meeting*

Jimmy Running Water drove his truck into the parking lot and parked next to a white SUV with its engine running. A man sat alone, smoking a cigarette in the dark. The only ambient light came from neighboring buildings.

Jimmy got out of his truck and approached the driver. "Are you Li?"

The man got out of the SUV. He was slender, medium height, with short grey hair, and wore black rim glasses. "You must be Running Water," He stated.

"Maybe, if your name is Li."

"I understand you and your partner have something for me," he said.

He sounds educated, Jimmy thought. "We do."

"I have a buyer for the antiquities. He'll be here on the eleventh. You'll receive the standard 2.9% fee. That's over ten thousand dollars each, for you and your associate, minus the one thousand dollars fee from each of you for my messenger."

A fee? The imposed fee did not sit well with Jimmy. "We were told we'd be getting ten thousand dollars each. There was no mention of a messenger's fee."

"That's the cost of doing business."

"We were promised ten thousand, and that's what we want," Jimmy insisted.

"You don't understand business. It's called paying commissions. That's what I'm doing, paying you a commission, and you have to pay a commission to the man who got you this job.

Jimmy sensed this man was attempting to cheat him. "That's not our problem!"

Li was growing impatient with this ignorant boy. "If it weren't for the messenger, you wouldn't get the job in the first place, and I'm sure nine thousand dollars is more than you have now. Just remember, I control all the money."

"You forget one thing, Li. You may control the money, but we control the masks; without them, you won't have any money to control. How's that for understanding business?"

Li realized the risk. He could lose the whole deal to this petty thief. "Don't be so rash. I'll tell you what. I will pay you the full commission, and you can pay the messenger yourself. How does that sound?" Li guessed that the messenger would never see the money from Jimmy and his partner, but they eventually would pay for that.

"That sounds like good business to me," Jimmy agreed.

"I want them delivered on the morning of the eleventh," Li said sternly. "The buyer will be here with cash. I'll send all the information . . . with the messenger." Li grinned.

A car passed by slowly heading west. Neither man spoke nor moved. The backlights turned into bright red lights when the passing car was about four blocks away.

"It stopped," Li said. "I think it's time for us to vanish."

Running Water rushed to his truck. He shifted into reverse, backed up, then shifted into first gear and sped away in the darkness with his headlights turned off.

## Chapter Eight

### First *Day*

Three days passed, and Milly sat on her rocking chair, puffing on her pipe, waiting. The sun had just risen above the horizon when Chile Charlie and Dolly arrived at the hogan as requested. Dolly hugged Charlie, wished him luck, and drove away in the El Camino. She had made copies of Google maps at the hotel and navigated her way to Interstate 40 and back to Gallup without a problem. Charlie brought a blanket from his hotel bed.

"That won't do," Milly told him. She walked into the hogan.

Shortly after, Nate Greystone came out carrying a large, thick wool Indian blanket—dark brown with rust stripes delineated with thin tan lines. "Here, this will keep you warm," Greystone said. "It's eighty-one years old. Grandmother made it when she was twelve." He traded blankets with Charlie.

Milly came out of the hogan holding the keys to her truck. "The lodge at Oak Creek is several miles away. We will have the purification ceremony there. Young Owl has already prepared the sweat lodge," Magi Milly said.

Greystone drove the truck while Charlie sat between him and Milly. Chile Charlie was a bit apprehensive and still uncertain about what would happen. He had expressed his grave concern to Dolly about the night before.

"You don't suppose they'll have me stand in the sun for twenty-four hours straight with just my skivvies on, stick eagle's talons and rock skewers through my chest skin, and then have me hanging to the lodge pole by leather straps, do you?" Charlie said.

Dolly broke into a burst of laughter. "Someone's been watching *A Man Called Horse* too many times." The laughter continued. "Oh, Charlie, it's just a purification ceremony to help you rid your mind of the 'bad spirits.' You're not taking a vow or becoming a warrior. Besides, the Sun Dance Ritual has been outlawed since 1883, and it was never a Navajo ritual. It was the Plains Indians."

Charlie felt embarrassed about his ignorance and lack of research on the topic. "Well, I still like to watch *A Man Called Horse*. It's a classic."

The three arrived at the base of the canyon, to an open area surrounded by dead juniper trees. The sweat lodge was a dome structure ten-foot in diameter and five-feet high made of mud and tree branches. The interior was completely dug out about a foot and a half deep and filled with river rock up to the ground level, except for a circular, two-foot opening in the center containing a firewood pile. The top surface of the piled rock was covered with dried mud, five inches deep, to protect a person from the hot rocks. A large wood tub, made from the bottom half of a wine barrel, filled with water from the Oak Creek, lay inside the lodge.

Greystone built a fire, and as the stones heated, he poured water over the hot rocks with a large wooden ladle. Steam began to rise. Meanwhile, Chile Charlie waited outside until Greystone was done with the preparations.

"If you are ready, we will begin with the purification ceremony. You'll need to bare off your clothing," Magi Milly explained.

Chile Charlie removed all his clothing, including a new pair of thermal long johns he wore over a black pair of jogging shorts, which he did not remove. Milly began the ritual with chants and songs, followed by prayers that symbolized the call to the Gods of the Four Directions. She sprayed Charlie with a special cleansing liquid composed of sage, water, and plants of the desert. She held burning sage before Charlie and told him to wave the smoke onto him.

"The entrance of the sweat lodge represents innocence and rebirth," Milly explained. "To enter the sweat lodge, you are required to get on your hands and knees as an act of humility while symbolically reentering the womb of our Great Mother Earth. Mother Earth knows your deepest wounds and needs and how to resolve them, and she requires absolute humility, vulnerability, and honesty."

Charlie entered the lodge alone on his hands and knees, then sat on the bare mud, a natural connection to Mother Earth herself. It was dark, and the only light came from the burning ambers and the hole in the ceiling for the smoke to escape. Milly picked up a door, a frame of tree branches covered with sheepskin, and placed it over the entrance.

"Keep pouring water on the rocks," Milly said to Charlie. She continued her chants as she pounded her staff on the red earth with a rhythmic beat, which made the jingle bells sound more like a tambourine, while Greystone beat on a small drum and chanted along.

Beads of sweat began to pour out of Charlie's body. He poured water over the rocks. Steam instantly filled the lodge with a thick mist. Sweat ran down his forehead and burned his eyes. He bent forward so the beads of sweat fell directly on the earth. The wide steam was almost suffocating, and he coughed. Exhaustion set in, and he felt like he was about to pass out. He concentrated on the chants, the beat of the drum, and the bells whir, which made him enter a state of euphoria.

Chile Charlie had no idea how long he had been in the lodge. His mind wandered in a dream-like state. He saw the buffalo, the Anasazi people, a lone coyote in the desert, and a wide river. Then he saw the snow in the desert and felt the chill of a cold winter.

"Charlie, it is time to come out," Milly said as she opened the door and let the cool air in.

Charlie came out, and the cool air felt good on his body. Greystone handed him a towel to dry off the sweat. Charlie dressed, Greystone extinguished the fire, and they left the sweat lodge site.

"Was that it?" Charlie asked.

"No. It is now time to start your journey," Milly said.

◆◆◆◆◆◆◆◆◆◆

They arrived at a canyon of red sandstone walls east of Navajo, New Mexico. They got out of the truck. Charlie looked at the land.

"The canyon is impressive," Charlie said in a hushed voice. "What's this place?"

"This is the land of the ancients who mysteriously disappeared from the desert. Much later, it became the land of our ancestors, the *Dine*. The ground is filled with their blood, and their spirits wander in this land.

"You must learn to avoid extremes. All does not exist," She said in a firm voice, "You must take the time to learn the intricacies and complexities of Mother Earth. This will take three days, and it starts here."

"The Navajo ritual, known as the *night chant*, is a healing ceremony lasting for three days and nights. It is performed in winter to restore the order and balance of human relationships within the Navajo universe. It includes praying, sacred dances, blessings, and chants. You will remain in this land of our ancestors, but you will not be alone. Mother Earth will be with you. Head into the canyon and wander the land. Observe the sky, the creatures, and the vegetation. Find the balance. It will help you find the peace and harmony you seek."

Milly walked to the truck and retrieved a leather bag from the back of the passenger's seat. She took out the sheath with the large Bowie knife and handed it to Charlie. "Take this. You will need it for your journey."

Charlie took the knife and glanced over to Greystone, who nodded approvingly.

"We will return to this spot four days from now."

"What am I supposed to do?" Charlie asked.

"Find a center and travel from there."

Charlie wasn't sure what that meant. Perhaps she was talking metaphorically, he thought.

Milly and Greystone left without another word, and Charlie was alone with Mother Earth.

▲▲▲▲▲

The canyon was spotted with melting snow from a previous snowfall that covered most of northern New Mexico at the higher elevations from Santa Fe to southern Colorado and barely touched west as far as Chinle, Arizona. It was already past noon when Charlie started on his journey. He walked down a slope to the flat land between two canyon walls. He wasn't sure what to do for the next three days and nights other than to 'become one with the earth.' His only certainty was finding a water source and a place to keep warm against the cold nights.

Water was the priority. Charlie knew a man could survive a week or more without food but only three days without water—a lesson he learned from his grandfather when Charlie was a young boy. For many years, during his youth, he and his grandfather camped in the wilderness during deer seasons. It was then that young Charlie learned survival skills—to hunt, find food from the land, make a fire, and most importantly, always find water first.

Worst case scenario, I can eat snow, Chile Charlie thought. He continued to walk northeast and occasionally looked back to mark his trail for his return to the rendezvous visually. After forty minutes of walking on the arid, rocky terrain, he finally finds his water source—a runoff of melting snow from the top of a mesa of Bowl Canyon down a gully. It was good, clean water. Charlie drank as much as his body could handle to keep him going until the next day. He decided to stay within close proximity of the gully and to venture just far enough without the risk of dehydration.

He continued to journey the canyon until he spotted a location on the southern slope. It was a shallow cove carved into the red sandstone by the winds of time, with a rocky overhang above that would protect it from the rain or snow. He climbed the slope to examine the cove. It wasn't large, but it was deep enough to protect him from the weather and maintain a fire that would radiate against the stone wall to keep him warm. The floor was solid sandstone, and the ceiling was nearly five feet high, not enough to stand in but sufficient to sit and sleep.

It was perfect, he thought — a place where he could hold out for three days.

Chile Charlie wiped the dust and small stones from the floor and placed the large wool blanket down. He walked down the slope and walked a distance, collecting dead branches from juniper pine trees and dried pinion leaves and pine needles. He collected a substantial pile to warm him well into the following day. He was getting hungry but was too tired to hunt for food.

He sat on the blanket, cut a notch into a thick tree branch with the Bowie knife, then stripped a thin branch and rounded the tip. He placed the stick into the notch and rubbed it back and forth between his palms. "It's an old Indian trick to start a fire," his grandfather had told Charlie. He kept rubbing for an extended amount of time. Finally, smoke. He placed a few dried leaves on top of the notch and continued to rub the thin branch on the log. Like a miracle, he had a fire. He added more dry twigs until he had a good fire going. The trick was to keep the ambers hot enough throughout the night to make it easier to start the next day's fire.

The cove warmed up. Charlie sat on the Indian blanket and watched the desert below. Three vultures circled over the canyon. A dead animal, Charlie thought. Darkness and cold set in early. Charlie sat on the edge of the large wool blanket, reached back, and pulled it over himself. It wasn't long before he closed his eyes and fell asleep sitting with his legs crossed.

## Chapter Nine

*Second Day*

Dolly Thompson drove to Albuquerque to meet with Dr. Levi Garcia, Professor of Southwestern Native American Studies at the University of New Mexico. It was 'Finals Week,' and she had only a few days before the university closed for the Christmas break.

She sat at his office and discussed possibly joining the archeological dig at Canyon de Chelly as an observer and conducting interviews for her book.

"I'm sorry, Miss Thompson, but that project has been shut down indefinitely," Dr. Garcia said.

"Why is that?"

"I am not at liberty to say, just that we encountered some difficulties that we have to sort out, but we can certainly accommodate you at Chaco Canyon."

Dolly was curious about Canyon de Chelly. Still, she was glad to be able to be part of the Chaco Canyon project. "Thank you, professor. I appreciate that."

"You're welcome. We're always happy to help a colleague interested in the Native American culture."

She changed the subject. "What do you make of this break-in at the Native American Museum in Gallup?

Professor Garcia raised an eyebrow at Dolly as if surprised by her question. "That is an odd case, a break-in without taking anything. I know the curator from there, Dr. Acothley. He is meticulous in his work. He would know immediately if any was missing."

"I suppose they're still checking their inventory to see if anything is missing," Dolly said.

"So, how are you enjoying the southwest so far? The professor asked.

Dolly told him about the attempted robbery on her first night and the carjacking the following morning.

"Don't you carry any protection with you," Dr. Garcia asked.

"No, I never needed to, and I'm from Chicago." She laughed.

"I guess you've already learned it's still the Wild West out here." He chuckled. "You know, there's a gun show here in town this weekend. You should probably go there. Maybe you'll find something that suits you."

▲▲▲▲▲

It was still dark when Charlie woke up to the sounds of chirping birds as if to announce the coming of Father Sun. He was lying on the ground feeling cold, the fire had gone out, but the occasional wind into the cove kept the ambers bright red.

Charlie grabbed a handful of thin twigs and dried leaves and placed them over the hot ambers. He blew on them until the leaves hissed into a flame. He put bigger branches on top and started a decent fire. Light began to silhouette the mountains to the east, and dark gray clouds began to take on a combination of lavender, mauve, and blue hues above the sun. The combination of the sunrise and the cool, fragrant desert air gave Charlie a strange sensation, but he would not move until it was warm enough to go out into the canyon. The clouds scudded away like ghosts, fading into nothing in the wind. Father Sun finally appeared.

He hadn't eaten in the past twenty-four hours, and the pain of hunger gnawed at his stomach. The Canyon was bleak and nearly bare of vegetation—no McDonalds. What could I round up to eat? Charlie gazed around. A lone eagle flew over the canyon to the east. Maybe it spotted some food. He threw more twigs into the fire to keep it going, then scuttled down the slope. Halfway down, he spotted a coyote heading east. Maybe it's going after the same food, he thought. The coyote stopped and turned its head in Charlie's direction. Charlie froze in place, hoping not to frighten it away. The coyote continued walking leisurely, not bothered by a man's presence. The eagle soared almost directly above Charlie. The coyote suddenly burst into a full run to the south and up a hill, where it stopped at the crest, turned to look at Charlie momentarily, and then disappeared over the hill. I must've scared it off, Charlie thought.

The cold yielded to the warmth of the sun. Charlie continued east on the sand and rocky terrain and walked around clumps of small pinyon junipers that looked more like bushes than trees. As he glanced up the canyon, a mountain cottontail rabbit took a startling dash from under a bush and ran north across Charlie's path. It hid under another Pinyon tree about fifty yards away. Charlie stopped for a moment. He followed the cotton tail slowly, but it ran farther away as Charlie approached. He could not get close enough to catch his breakfast. If I miss this one, I might go hungry for the rest of the day or days.

The rabbit ran towards the north wall of the canyon. Charlie thought that if I could get him to run to the wall, he'll have only two ways he could go. The rabbit headed for the canyon wall and stopped to figure out his next move. Charlie picked up a rock the size of a baseball and continued toward his prey. The rabbit ran east along the wall past an enormous Pinyon tree in front of the wall. Charlie estimated his windage, threw the rock as hard as possible, and struck the back of the rabbit's head. It continued for a few feet and then balled up and squirmed. Charlie ran behind the rabbit's trail. His eyes were focused on the squirming creature, and he did not see the two bowling ball size rocks on the ground before him. He tripped, flew forward, and crashed on the graveled ground. As is human nature, he looked back to see what caused his fall. He thought the two rocks looked out of place. At least I got my usual run this morning, he thought.

He got up, breathing hard, and walked to the motionless rabbit—it was dead.

Charlie picked up his breakfast and walked back to the unusual rocks. He didn't know what to make of them. Was it some marker? Indians were known to mark their trails, but he was no trail. Charlie squatted next to the rocks and examined them. One had crusted red dirt embedded in the crevices on the top side. He stood up and searched the nearby area. He found two impressions on the ground where the rocks once rested. From where he stood and from the direction of the sunlight, he noticed the difference in the top soils. It was less grainy around the rocks than the rest of the terrain. He examined the ground around the rocks. It softer. Something has been recently buried here, he thought. He left the area to prepare breakfast but planned to return to the two rocks later.

To avoid uninvited wildlife and insects where he sleeps, Charlie removed the entrails and skinned the rabbit before he returned to his cove. He gathered extra wood for his campfire. He skewered the rabbit with a long, thin, and almost straight branch and placed the ends on stacked flat sandstone rocks, which he happened to put on opposite sides of the fire so the rabbit would cook above the flame. Chile Charlie took his time to roast his lunch. He knew two things about the desert rabbit—never eat them before the first frost, and rabbit meat needs to cook for at least two hours. The frost kills the fleas and ticks that carry Lyme disease, and they will not taste gamey and leathery if simmered.

The first bite of the rabbit was not what he expected. A bit tough, but it kept him nourished. Charlie kept thinking about the strange rocks he tripped over and wondered what was beneath the ground. It couldn't be a sacred burial ground. The hole appeared to be square-shaped and not rectangular. It couldn't be a body, and it couldn't be ancient because it was freshly dug. The thoughts about the strange hole fed his curiosity while the cooked rabbit fed his body.

He ate half of the rabbit and thought to save the other half for the next day. He took it further up to the top of the slope, where there were large patches of snow. Charlie built a mound of snow, placed the remaining rabbit on top, and built another large pile of snow over it. With his Bowie knife, he cut several branches of juniper with leaves and placed them over his mount of snow. He hoped a coyote, bobcat, or mountain lion wouldn't discover tomorrow's breakfast.

He was sure he could locate the two strange rocks again, but he had to return to the gully to fill himself with enough water to hold him over for another day.

▲▲▲▲▲

Charlie got on his hands and knees and examined the ground. Yes, someone recently dug this hole here, but why, and what? "We're about to find out," he said.

Charlie looked for a large flat sandstone rock for digging. He found one and pounded a beveled edge on one side for digging and scooping.

The deeper he dug, the softer the soil. He searched and scooped until he was a foot down—nothing. He continued to dip. Two feet deep and still nothing. The sun was warming, and Chile Charlie began to perspire. He removed his coat and proceeded to dig and scoop. Three feet into the hole, and still, there was nothing.

"This must be something large and serious," Charlie said. He was sweating profusely. His breathing was heavy, and he sat for a rest. He was glad he drank much water. Still, he wished he had a canteen. A prickly pear margarita sounded good about then. He dug again. His sweat dripped into the soil, his shoulder and arm muscles began to burn, and his palms began to blister. Charlie was persistent. He scraped with the flat rock and lifted loose dirt out of the hole with cupped hands until, finally, a black cloth appeared. He stood up to catch his breath and scanned his surroundings to ensure no one was watching. He looked at the sky, hoping for clouds, but all he saw in the pale blue was the eagle soaring high above him. Maybe he's thinking of making a meal of me, Charlie thought.

To avoid damage to whatever was down there, he carefully dug around the cloth with his hands and scooped the dirt away methodically like a professional archeologist. Within moments he located the collar of a black cloth sack, wrapped tightly with a long and thin leather strap. He dug along the sides and soon discovered it was a large sack. He scooped dirt out until he could lift the bag from the hole by its collar. He untied the strap and looked inside and saw some things individually wrapped in red velvet cloth. He took one from the bag and unfolded the fabric. It was an antiquated

Kachina mask made of old dried leather, painted in several colors that have long lost their luster.

A sense of excitement came over him, as well as a sense of fear. Many thoughts whirled in his head like dirt devils, mainly because he had broken a taboo law. Is this something man was not meant to find, he thought. He felt a sudden sense that someone was watching him. He looked in all directions, but there was no one — only the eagle above him.

Charlie wrapped the mask and placed it back in the bag. This is nothing mystical, he thought. These are just stolen relics, most likely from the museum. He recalled, from the news, that no items were reported missing. Charlie covered the hole and placed the original rocks over it. He carried the sack away, along with his digging rock, back to his cove.

The gully still ran with clear water, and Charlie drank as much as possible to replace what he had lost that morning. He decided to hide the black sack somewhere near the gully as it was closer to the trail where Milly was to pick him up.

Charlie searched the area for an inconspicuous hiding place. He decided that the best site would be up on the slope. He spotted a good location, behind the third juniper tree west of the gully. Charlie carefully removed rocks and dug a shallow hole wide and deep enough for easy recovery. He covered the hole with moist soil and spread dry dirt for concealment. He placed the original rocks over the hole — it looked untouched. No one would suspect that hiding behind a tree, up on a slope, is a hole containing valuable Indian artifacts. He drank more cool water and returned to his cove.

## Chapter Ten

*Third Day*

Charlie woke up hungry and tired but decided not to eat the rabbit again. Let nature have that rabbit, he thought. He returned to the gully and discovered it was drying up. The warm sun had melted away most of the snow from the top of the mesa. There was still some water to drink, but there might be none by tomorrow. He thought Milly would be here in twenty-four hours to pick me up and return me to civilization.

Chile Charlie spends his last day walking about the desert. He appreciated the beauty of the sky, the land formations, the flora, and what little wildlife he saw—mostly lizards and a few ground squirrels that came out to bask in the sun's warmth. What am I doing here? What is it that I am supposed to see that would make my life clear, he wondered. In the evening, he gathered dry wood and returned to his cove.

The canyon began to cool. He started a campfire near the edge of the overhang above the cove. He sat close to the fire, wrapped with the old Indian blanket hooded over his head. He thought about the black sack and the Kachina masks. Where did they come from? Who hid them in the canyon, and why? Should I report him to the police? What if the feds take them just like they confiscated the T-Rex fossil from the Lakota tribe in South Dakota? It was never seen again. Those masks belong to the people of the local tribes.

Magi Milly would return in twelve hours. He was there to learn about the Navajo Way, not to retrieve lost treasures. Should I tell her about my find or hide it from Magi? Although he had secured the Kachina masks, he needed to figure out if he was doing the right thing. He grew exhausted and didn't think about it any longer. He waited for the early sunset of late fall and observed the canyon silently, without motion. He returned to his cove and fell asleep.

▲▲▲▲▲

Chile Charlie woke up as the bright sun peeked out of the eastern sky. He was anxious to leave the canyon. He cleaned out the cove and left no trace that he had been there. He rolled up his blanket and walked past the gully. It was dry.

Magi Milly and Greystone waited in the truck, and he was happy to see them. Greystone handed him a jug of fresh water from Oak Creek, which Charlie almost emptied with large gulps. The return trip to the hogan was quiet. Milly didn't ask about his experience, and Greystone just smiled.

They arrived at Milly's home, where Dolly waited by the El Camino. She had a pleasant smile. "Hello, Chile Charlie,"

"How are you, Dolly?"

"I'm glad you're back safe and sound. Are you okay?" Dolly asked. "I bet you're ready to return to the hotel for a hot shower and lunch."

Charlie nodded eagerly. "Yes, I want a shower, food, and a soft bed, in that order."

Charlie shook hands with Nate Greystone. He turned to Milly.

"Thank you, Magi Milly. I will never forget this experience." He handed the Bowie knife back to her.

"Goodbye, Chile Charlie. Go home and rest," Milly said. She walked into the hogan without another word.

Charlie and Dolly drove away.

"How was your experience in the canyon?"

"Dolly, you will not believe what I found." He told her about accidentally tripping over the two rocks and discovering a hidden treasure.

## Chapter Eleven

*Strange Friends*

John Trefren sat at the El Ranch Hotel restaurant having breakfast with his old friend, Russell Strongbow, reminiscing and laughing about their youth's mischief, some of which amounted to petty crimes.

"Remember when officer Kelso ran after those kids at the shopping center? He left his police car running with the flashing red and blue overhead lights, and you went to his car and locked it. We sat in your GTO and watched old "Fat" Kelso run back to get into his car, and he couldn't get in!" Russell broke into loud laughter.

"I was just a punk juvenile back then. I'm just lucky I never got caught," Trefren said.

"I can't believe you did all those things back then, Tre," Russell Strongbow said, shaking his head. "And here you are, a detective with the Gallup Police Department."

Trefren was a medium size man, about five-foot-nine, with deep-set eyes, on his narrow oval face. A few strands of gray highlighted his thick dark hair. He was a fifteen-year veteran of the Gallup Police Department — the last nine years spent as a detective working in the Felony Crimes Division. Only relatives and close friends called him *Tre*. He was from the Ramah Navajo Reservation south of Gallup.

His friend, Russell Strongbow, was from the neighboring Zuni reservation south of Gallup. He was a tall, barrel-chested, and muscular man with long black hair split in the center and always wore a broad red headband to hold it in place, which made him look more Apache than Zuni. Russell was proud of his body and wore tight-fitted shirts to show off his muscular physic and jeans so tight against his body that it left little to the imagination.

The two had been friends since childhood, and even though Russell served five years in the State penitentiary in Santa Fe for armed robbery and assault with a deadly weapon, they continued as close friends.

"So, Russ, what did you want to see about? Trefren asked.

"I'm missing some sheep and a few goats, and I think I know who the thieves are. It's that Nate

Greystone and his two buddies, Jimmy Running Water and Chris Leaping Bear," Russell said, pounding his forefinger on the table.

"What makes you believe they're responsible," Trefren asked.

"Everyone knows they're the biggest thieves in the whole county. Not only that, but I have also seen them near my ranch. They have no business on the Zuni reservation. I know they were out here scouting my ranch, and now I'm missing some livestock. Damn Navajos!" Strongbow roared.

"Calm down, Russ. Have you contacted the Zuni Police? That's their jurisdiction."

"I don't trust them. That's why I'm telling you this, Tre. I know Jimmy is your cousin. Maybe you can get him to fess up against the other two, and I won't press charges against him, but I will against the other two punks."

"I'll admit, my cousin Jimmy will never win the *Citizen of the Year Award,* and Leaping Bear is about as dumb as they come, but Nate, he's a good kid with bad friends and a lot smarter than Jimmy or Chris. Out of the three, he's the only one with a job, delivering propane. He's been questioned a few incidents, but he's clean."

"Maybe too smart to get caught, John. I hate those Navajos."

"I'll talk to my cousin, see what he knows, and speak with Nate. And remember this, Russell, I'm Navajo."

Strongbow had always been outspoken about his dislike of the Navajo people. "You're a Ramah Navajo, an outcast like me. That's why you and I have always gotten along," Strongbow said.

▲▲▲▲▲

Dolly tapped her fingers on the table while waiting for Charlie to arrive. She noticed the two men sitting across the room as they laughed loudly. One was tall, dark, and muscular, with an opened shirt collar exposing his smooth chest. He liked his jewelry, Dolly thought. He wore a leather necklace with a single sizeable turquoise stone shaped like an arrowhead and a silver ring with multiple colored stones on almost every finger. The other man wore blue jeans, a western sports jacket, and a navy blue Polo shirt. He was shorter than the muscular man and had a lighter complexion, but Native American and not ornate and ostentatious as his friend.

Charlie walked into the restaurant past the two men and sat beside Dolly at the square dining table.

"That man over is a police officer," Charlie said as he cocked his head toward the two men at the table.

"Which one?"

"The one that doesn't need all the attention. I saw the badge case he was wearing on his belt. Looks like he's got a gun under that coat too."

"I bet you're starving, Charlie." She smiled.

"I'm going to order everything on the menu except for rabbit."

Dolly laughed. "Don't worry. I don't think they serve rabbit here."

Charlie leaned closer to Dolly. "What do you think I should do about the masks?" he asked in a hushed voice.

"I'm not sure. They're still claiming nothing has been taken from the Navajo Art Museum," Dolly said in almost a whisper.

"But don't you find it curious? Two men assault a security guard, enter the museum, and take nothing?"

"I'm sure the police are working on that now."

Charlie leaned back on his chair. "I'm going to find out. Come on, let's go to my room and order room service."

As they walked out, Charlie surprised Dolly when he approached the table with the two men.

"Sorry to bother you, but are you a police officer," he asked the man wearing the sports jacket.

"Yes, I'm detective John Trefren with the Gallup Police Department," he said politely. "This is my friend Russell Strongbow, a resident from here."

Strongbow greeted them with a nod. He smiled at Dolly.

"I'm Charlie, and this is Dolly. I was just wondering if they caught any suspects yet and if anything was stolen from the museum."

Strongbow's smile vanished, and they looked at Charlie with curiosity. "Why do you want to know," he asked.

"Just curious. I am interested in Native American culture, and Dolly here is an anthropologist."

"We're still working on the case," Detective Trefren informed them.

"Okay, thank you for your time," Charlie said directly to Trefren.

Charlie called for room service to his room. He ordered more food than he thought he could handle.

"You think we should let the police know about those masks?" Dolly asked.

Charlie had concerns about the valid owner of the Kachina masks. "They may not have come from the museum, Dolly. Let us wait."

"Then I think we should go and get those masks before someone else finds them, or worse yet, the person who hid them may return to get them, and we'll never see them again. But if we retrieve them, I'm sure someone will be distraught when they discover they're gone. Then we'll know who hid them there."

"That's what I'm afraid of," Charlie said.

▲▲▲▲▲

It was barely dusk when Chile Charlie parked the El Camino on the dirt trail where Magi Milly had dropped him off a few days before. Dolly wanted to go with him, but Charlie insisted there were too many dangers in that canyon, especially in the dark.

"It's best to wait here in the car," Charlie advised. "Tribal Police is patrolling the area, so keep the engine running, lights off, and don't step on the brakes, or you'll light up the desert, and they'll spot us from miles away,"

"Are you sure you don't want me to come?" Dolly was a bit apprehensive about being left alone in the dark.

"You'll be okay. Keep the doors locked, and remember, my gun is in the glovebox with a round in the chamber and the safety off. It's ready to go. Just don't shoot until you're sure it's not me." Charlie disappeared in the darkness carrying a flashlight and his hiking stick.

He kept the flashlight down at a sharp angle, just enough to see in front of him. He walked along the base of the southern slope, where he knew he'd find the narrow gully. Charlie walked for nearly forty minutes before he found it. He turned the light off, stood motionless, and listened for any unusual noises, mostly humankind. He heard none. Charlie shined his flashlight up the slope and to the right until he spotted the juniper.

Dolly remained in the car, nervously alert. It seemed as if she had been waiting for hours. She heard a startling cracking noise from outside. Dolly couldn't see anything. She opened the glovebox and took out the .380 Beretta. She heard it again, approaching the passenger side of the car. She held the gun in both hands and pointed the muzzle toward the passenger window. Then, a light flashed on the ground and rapidly zigzagged in many directions. The light went up and shone on a man's face—it was Charlie. Dolly exhaled and realized she had been holding her breath.

Charlie kept the light on himself. "It's me, Dolly, don't shoot," he said as he approached the car. Charlie walked to the back of the car and unzipped his large suitcase. He removed all his clothes, placed the black sack into it, placed his clothing on top of the bag, and zipped up the suitcase.

▲▲▲▲▲

He took the masks from the black sack and laid them across his bed.

"My God, Charlie. We are in trouble. These are actual Anasazi Kachina masks. These are worth the money. But who buried them in that canyon?"

"That's the whole mystery, Dolly."

"What are we going to do?"

"We're going to hide them, but first, I am taking pictures." Charlie took several photographs of the masks with his cell Phone. "I'm going to the public copier in the lobby and printing some copies. Wait here. I'll be right back." He left carrying his backpack and returned twenty minutes later.

Dolly was worried. She didn't expect that something like this would land on their laps. "I know a man at the University of New Mexico who's an expert in southwestern Native American culture. I think he can help us. His name is Dr. Levi Garcia.

"Don't you think he'll become suspicious, especially if he's an expert? He'll ask too many questions we don't want to answer."

"What's your plan, then?"

Charlie hesitated to answer. He did want to hurt her feelings, but it was necessary. "I can't tell you, Dolly. The less you know, the less you'll be in trouble if things go wrong.

## Chapter Twelve

*Evil Christmas Spirits*

"Let's go open our Christmas present," Running Water quipped. He smiled anxiously like a little boy waiting for Santa Clause.

"Do you think the heat's off yet," Chris Leaping Bear asked.

"It's been two weeks now, and there's nothing new on the radio. I don't think they know about the masks. I think it's time." Jimmy said. "Go get the shovels and flashlights." He said as he searched for the key to his pickup truck.

Chris hurried to do as Jimmy ordered.

"Don't forget the whiskey and be quick about it. I don't want to waste any more time here. We're going to be rich!" Running Water exclaimed.

It was a moonless night as the boys drove back to the canyon. They were in merry spirits with laughter and song. They hadn't drunk yet. The whiskey was for celebration after the retrieval of their treasure. The boys sang "Jingle Bells" at the top of their lungs until they arrived at the canyon.

The site was more challenging to find than the merry boys thought. They scanned slowly with flashlights searching for over an hour in the cold. They finally found the large juniper three and the two large rocks. Jimmy noticed that the two rocks appeared to have been moved. No coyote could have moved them, he thought. Worry set in, then anger, and then fear. Someone knows we've been here, he thought.

Leaping Bear dug and dug while Running Water held the flashlights. He reached the bottom of the hole—no sack. That was Jimmy's fear.

"What happened to our treasure?" Leaping Bear shouted, "Somebody stole our masks!"

Running Water remained silent, looking down into the hole. His eyes burned with anger as his mind dug for answers.

"What are we going to do? Those masks belong to us, Jimmy. We've got to find them!" Leaping Bear exclaimed.

"Shut up and let me think!" There was silence. Running Water thought. "Let's go pay a visit to the medicine woman. She knows everything that goes on in the canyon. I bet she knows who's been out here, and I bet she knows about the masks too . . . I know she does."

"We can't do that tonight. It's too late, and we don't want to upset her," Leaping Bear said. "Let's go back to Gallup and come back in the morning to see Milly," he suggested.

They drove away in poor spirits, this time without song. It was a silent night.

Jimmy and Chris were up and ready to go in the dark morning. Though they were tired from the long drive home, neither had a restful night. Jimmy spent the night thinking about all the trouble they had gone through—the museum, the burial of the masks, the retrieval, and now, they wake up empty-handed in Gallup, New Mexico.

"It is too early to go see Milly," Chris said. He feared upsetting the older woman.

"No, it's not. That witch never sleeps, and I want to get those masks back before it's too late." Jimmy said with anger. They were in trouble. The meeting with the buyer was taking place that afternoon.

▲▲▲▲▲

Milly's walked outside to the cool, fresh desert air and sat on her rocking chair every morning. The light began to glow behind the mountains on the eastern horizon. She sat motionless and listened to the desert, wrapped in an old wool blanket of faded earth colors. Her excellent great-grandmother had woven that blanket back when the Navajo fought to preserve their freedom. It was passed on to Milly only to fight against the cold.

The sun rose above the horizon, and the silence was broken by the sound of an approaching truck that could be heard from a far distance. She recognized that sound.

"Good morning Milly," Running Water said as he exited the truck. "Is Nate here?"

"No, he left for town again," Milly said.

By the scowl on her face, Jimmy knew she was already upset. "Do you have time to talk to us? We want to ask you a few questions."

"It depends on the questions," Milly answered.

"Have you noticed any strange people coming around the canyon lately, maybe tourists or hikers?"

Milly noticed Leaping Bear sitting in the truck, and it appeared he was not getting out. "I know the spirits in the canyon have been disturbed." She glace back at Running Water. "Why do you ask?" Milly said with cynical eyes. "Did you lose something out there?"

"No reason in particular. We were just curious. We thought that we could get jobs as guides." Does she know what we've been doing down there? Running Water wondered. "We just wanted to know if there'd been anyone out there, you know, to help them in case they got lost," he said.

"The Spirits tell me that only noisy demons have been down there. Maybe they have sent the *spirit coyote* to expel the demons from the canyon," she said.

Running Water didn't know what to make of that. "Bueno, we'll leave you in peace to watch the sun do its thing or whatever you do," he said disrespectfully. He turned and looked about at Milly's place as if he was looking for something or perhaps scheming.

"What are you looking for?" Milly asked as she pushed the blanket away in front of her. "I told you, Young Owl is not here."

Jimmy froze, staring at a .45 Colt revolver in an old, worn-out, brown leather cross-draw holster on Milly's belt. She's old, maybe too weak to lift the gun or pull the trigger, Jimmy thought, but this was not a good time to find out. Without another word, he turned slowly and got into the pickup truck. They drove away, leaving a cloud of red dust that could be seen for several miles.

"What did Milly tell you?" Leaping Bear asked.

"Nothing! Just her crazy talk about spirits. That old witch!" Jimmy didn't mention Milly's revolver. He pounded the steering wheel with his fist. "Our buyer is coming to Gallup today. We gotta find those masks soon." Jimmy understood the severity of their situation if they were to show up at the meeting empty-handed.

"What are we going to do now," Chris asked.

Jimmy had thought about tying the older woman and searching the entire place for the black sack, but the rumor about Milly was confirmed, she did carry a gun. As far back as Jimmy could remember, there were stories about the old medicine woman and how deadly she was with a six-shooter. It was said that Magi Milly once shot and killed a man for trying to steal her sheep. She buried him in the desert; the body was never found, but that was only a rumor. When Nate moved in with his grandmother, the other children asked him if the stories about Milly were true. Nate neither confirmed nor denied the rumors.

Jimmy was becoming desperate. "She knows something, won't talk, but I know someone who will."

▲▲▲▲▲

Nate Greystone drove Milly's truck to the village of Crystal to pick up the propane truck for an early morning service at one of the remote ranches. Cell phone reception was better in Crystal, and Nate could read all the messages. One of the text messages read:

*Meet me by the entrance at the airport.*

After the propane service, Nate returned the propane truck to the company yard and headed south for the airport near Gallup in Milly's truck.

## Chapter Thirteen

*Land of the People*

It was midmorning when Charlie arrived at Milly's house. He noticed her pickup truck was not there and wondered if anyone was home. He stepped out of his truck anyway.

Milly appeared at the door. "Chile Charlie, I saw you in my dream that you would come here today to tell me something important." She motioned him to enter.

Charlie walked in with his backpack and placed it on the table. "Good morning, Milly."

"You want some coffee to wake your spirit?"

Charlie gave her a single nod.

"What troubles you, Chile Charlie?

"I have something I want to show you." He reached into the backpack, took out several sheets of paper, and handed them to Milly.

She studied the photos briefly, then placed them on the table and sat down. Milly lighted her pipe and blew the smoke up, creating a hazy cloud.

"The ancients were the farming tribes who lived in the dwellings of the mountains." She pointed to the pictures. "These are the masks of the Kachinas. They were benevolent beings from the underworld. They appeared before the ancients and danced to make rain for their crops. But the enemy of the ancients killed the Kachinas, and their spirits were sent to dwell at the bottom of the desert lake for eternity, but they left masks, in their image, in the desert for the people to find. The Spirit of the Kachinas is in the masks, and those who wear them will become the embodiment of the Kachinas, and they too can make rain."

Milly looked hard into Charlie's eyes. "Where did you find these pictures, Chile Charlie?

He hesitated to say, but her stare was too intense. She may already know the truth, he thought. Charlie told her how he found the black sack buried in the canyon.

"What will you do with them," Milly asked.

"Well, there are no reports of missing Kachina masks from the break-in of the museum in Gallup, and there aren't any claims from the owner anywhere in the news or the internet. I'd hate for them to end up in the wrong hands."

"Those masks belong to the desert, not in a museum..."

"And not in the federal government archives," Charlie inserted.

"Charlie, I am worried about Young Owl. He's gone again. I rode my horse out this morning after sunrise, and when I returned, he was gone. He left me a note that he was going into Crystal for a propane service and would then return" She took a small blue piece of paper out the pocket of her wool sweater and placed it on the table."

"May I see that?" Charlie asked.

Milly pushed the note to Charlie. He unfolded the note and read it."

"Where do you think he went?

"He likes to go visit with his friends with bad spirits. He goes to a house called Blackrock's. It is just an old house belonging to Sam Blackrock. It's a hideaway in the hills south of Gallup, maybe five or seven miles. Not a good place."

"I'll go look for him." Charlie reached to take the photos, but Milly grabbed them quickly. She went to the iron cooking stove, opened the firebox door, and threw the sheets of paper into the burning wood. "These were not meant for one to see, she said."

Charlie looked at her blankly for a moment, then nodded in agreement.

"Be careful, Chile Charlie. There is nothing there but black hearts. Charlie left and sat in his car for a moment. He watched Milly walk behind the house toward the stable.

## Chapter Fourteen

*Perea Corrals*

Stephan Giles rode comfortably in the back seat of a black Chevy Suburban. It wasn't the trip from Albuquerque International Airport that bothered him. It was the desolate land of truck stops, red hills, lava rock, semi-trucks, and wide open space of nothingness. It was nothing like Dallas, Texas, where he flew in a company jet. He carried a tan, hard leather travel bag, hand-tooled with the circle star, long horns, the Texas flag, and barbed wire patterns that made it look like a fancy saddle. The travel bag was pure Texas, and it held oil money.

Giles dressed like a Texan with a charcoal gray western suit, a white dress shirt with a bolo tie, a shiny silver belt buckle, and polished black boots. He had reddish-blonde hair under a black Stetson hat, and mysterious eyes were hidden behind a pair of Oakleys. He was the runner for his boss, a millionaire oil man, buyer, and collector of rare southwestern antiquities, most obtained illegally. He was accompanied by his assistant and driver, Simon, a six-foot, two-inch tall ex-Texas Ranger.

The Suburban arrived at *Perea*, a place with a name, but no town, only the *Iyanbito* Gospel Lighthouse Church. Simon drove north of the freeway on an isolated dirt road that led to the abandoned corrals, where they parked and waited.

Stephan patted the tan leather bag resting next to him. It contained $500,000 in one-hundred-dollar bills. "Simon, when he arrives, get out and just stand by the door," he told his driver. There was no drawl to his voice, more upper Midwest than Texan.

Five minutes later, a white KIA SUV arrived and stopped about thirty feet away, facing the front of the black Suburban. The driver and passenger doors opened simultaneously. The driver exited the vehicle.

Giles exited his vehicle and left the leather bag in the back seat. He motioned the driver of the KIA to step closer. They met in the middle between the two facing cars.

"Hello, Mr. Giles. Good to see you again."

"Hello, Lee. Do you have the goods?"

"They will be here shortly." Although the notion of going home with half a million dollars excited him, Lee's nervous voice betrayed him. He had not heard from Jimmy Running Water, who had also not answered the multiple calls made to his phone.

"You mean, you arrived here without the merchandise?" Mr. Giles said.

"I can assure you, the carrier will arrive here shortly," Lee explained.

"Lee, I'm a patient man, so I'll give your carrier twenty minutes, and that's all."

Mr. Giles returned to the suburban and sat in the back seat. "Simon, when I get out of the car, make the call."

Lee returned to his KIA and slammed the door. "Call Jimmy again and find out where the hell he is!" He said to his passenger.

Twenty minutes passed, and the masks did not arrive.

"Lee, are you playing me?"

"No, Mr. Giles. We don't know what happened to the man supposed to meet us here."

Stephan Giles puts his arm around Lee's shoulders as if they were pals. "Lee, we've done business together many times in the past. This is the first time you've disappointed us."

"But Mr. Giles, you don't understand . . ."

"I understand that you have lost control here." He glanced at Lee's SUV. "And you brought some muscle with you?"

"You've brought muscle too, Mr. Giles," Lee said with a subtle tone of insolence.

"I've got five hundred thousand dollars to protect. You have nothing." Mr. Giles said emphatically. He turned to look at his driver.

Simon shook his head with subtle motions.

"I'm sorry, Lee. I'm afraid we will no longer require your services. Please take us off your contact list." Stephan Giles sharply and returned to the black Suburban.

"Wait! Mr. Giles, I can get those masks to you," Lee shouted.

The black suburban sped away and covered Lee in a cloud of dust. Lee returned to his white SUV.

"I want you to find this Jimmy Running Water," Lee said furiously. "Get the masks back. And take care of him. I don't care what you must do. Do you get me?" Lee said, pointing his finger at his passenger.

"I get you, Lee, but it's not just Jimmy I have to take care of. There are two others, and that will cost you extra," Russell Strongbow said.

## Chapter Fifteen

*Braided Tail*

Nate Greystone arrived at Blackrock's and parked next to Jimmy Running Water's truck. It was quiet except for the closing of the driver's door. Too early for these bums to be up, Nate thought. Before he reached the three steps to the porch deck, the front door flew open. Jimmy walked out with Chris trailing behind.

"Where've you been? Jimmy shouted.

"I've been looking for you all morning," Nate said as he reached into his outer coat pocket. "I have a message for you." He handed the note to Jimmy.

Jimmy yanked the blue paper out of Nate's hand and read the message.

*Iyanbito church, n .3 mi, left .2 mi to Perea corrales, 1pm*

"A bit too late." Jimmy crumbled the note and tossed it on the front seat of his truck through the opened passenger window. "We've been looking for you too." He grabs Greystones by the coat and pulls him in close. "Okay, shrimp, I want to know where my masks are, or I will tear your limbs from your body,"

"What masks? I don't even know what you're talking about."

"You know what I'm talking about, the sack with the four Kachina masks," Jimmy said.

"The ones you stole from us from the canyon!" Chris Leaking Bear shouted from the porch.

"We know you took the sack, and I want it back now!" Jimmy demanded.

Nate grabbed Jimmy's wrists and shoved him back. "I don't have your damn masks. I didn't take them."

"Well, if you didn't take them, then only one other person could have taken them, your grandmother. She told us that she knew we'd been in the canyon."

Nate began to worry. "When did she tell you that?"

"We visited her this morning when we looked for you. Maybe we'll go back and visit the old witch, only this time she'll give us our masks, or I will take her scalp. That should be worth some money."

Jimmy had never called Milly an 'old witch,' and it infuriated him that his friend threatened to harm his grandmother. He cocked his right hand back and struck Jimmy on the left side of his face with a punch that sent him flying onto the porch steps.

"If ever come near our house again, I will kill you and bury you in the desert where no one will ever find you." Nate knew he had a tough fight coming. Jimmy was slightly taller, broader, and stronger.

Jimmy got up slowly. "Greystone, maybe we should call you *Yellowstone* instead. You were always a coward. You never got caught, and we were the ones who always went to jail."

"That's because you're stupid, and your yellow dog here." He pointed at Chris.

Jimmy pulled a knife with a seven-and-a-half-inch blade from the leather sheath on his belt. "Big words from a little man," Jimmy said.

Nate removed his coat, threw it on the ground, reached behind him, and drew his Bowie knife with the fourteen-inch blade. "Big knife for a big man," Nate responded.

Jimmy's eyes widened, and Leaping Bear's jaw dropped open. Neither of them had seen that knife before, just as they had never seen the medicine bag Nate had always carried.

"Don't think about it, Jimmy," Nate warned. "My grandfather was the best knife fighter on the reservation. I carry his blood, and you're not that good."

"Teach him a lesson, Jimmy!" Chris shouted from the porch, careful to keep his distance from the knives.

Jimmy approached Nate, crouched with feigning movements. Nate remained calm, holding his knife in his right hand with the blunt side down. Jimmy lunged at Nate for a stab to the stomach. With the blunt side of the Bowie knife, Nate struck down on Jimmy's wrist and instantly swung the blade up and across Jimmy's upper chest, cutting his plaid shirt and black-hooded jacket. Jimmy felt an instant stream of current numbing rush up his arm, almost making him drop his knife. He stepped back and looked at his chest—no blood.

Jimmy charged at Nate with wild, slashing swings. Nate avoided the sharp blade with dodges and shifting movements without overreacting. Jimmy swung for a cross slash. In two quick moves, Nat struck the wrist with the blunt end again and turned back across Jimmy's face while simultaneously grappling the knife-wielding wrist. It was only a surface cut to the right side of the face. Jimmy dropped the knife as he stepped away from his opponent. Nate kicked Jimmy's groin with the force of a wild mustang. Jimmy bowed over on his knees. Nate walked behind him and kicked his back, sending Jimmy's face to the ground.

Nate straddled Jimmy's back. "I'm not going to kill you, but I am taking your scalp. You don't deserve to go to the spirit world. With his left hand, Nate grabbed a hand full of hair. He yanked the head back and placed the sharp blade at the top of the forehead.

"Nate, don't do it!" Chris Leaping Bear yelled.

Nate closed his eyes, tilted his head back, gave out Indian whoops, and shouted, *"Nílch'i!"* With one quick movement, Nate made a slashing cut. "I will hang this in my hogan," Nate declared as he held the long braided ponytail up.

Jimmy moaned as he came back to a higher level of consciousness.

"Waste Water. The next time you show up to my house, I will have my grandmother put a spell on you, and you'll be crapping horned toads for the rest of your wasted life . . . and that's going to hurt every time.

Nate picked up Jimmy's knife and walked to the porch, where Chris squatted with teary eyes. "Where's your knife?"

"I don't have one," Chris said shakenly.

Nate dropped Jimmy's knife in front of the frightened boy. "Here, this is yours now. Maybe you'll be wiser with it. Nate walked down the steps, stopped, and turned. "You know, Chris. Just because you raise sheep doesn't mean you have to be one. Become a mountain lion, and I'll stop calling you *Leaking* Bear." Nate took the braided ponytail and placed it in his medicine bag.

▲▲▲▲▲

Dolly was about to finish her coffee when she saw Nate Greystone enter the hotel lobby. She left her table to greet him. "Nate, what are you doing here?"

He was caught by surprise. "I'm looking for Charlie."

"He's not here right now."

Dolly thought Nate looked like he'd been in a fight. "He won't be here for a while, but if you want to wait for him, I'll buy you breakfast or lunch. Come on,"

Dolly noticed the concerned look on the boy. She saw him as a boy, but he wasn't. He was built like a man, about five nine, slender body with broad shoulders, which indicated he was a hard physical worker. He had large brown eyes under the prominent superciliary arches and smooth skin on his oval face. Perhaps it was the look on his face, an innocence behind those angry eyes. His long hair was split in the center and pulled back in a ponytail. He wore tan canvas pants and a black pullover wool sweater under a faded olive drab army field jacket. It was as if he tried not to look Native American.

"How did you know to find Charlie here," Dolly asked.

"I saw his tan and turquoise car parked in the parking lot a few days ago. I just figured he stays here."

Dolly told him about her background and why she was in Gallup. She was curious about this troubled young man. "What's it like living here in Gallup?"

"I didn't grow up here. My parents sent me here to live with my grandparents." He cast his eyes down almost in shame, admitting he was unwanted by his family. "They thought the demon spirits possessed me. They figured my grandmother could heal me. I've only been here seven years."

"Did it work? Did your grandmother heal you?"

"Dolly, I don't have evil spirits, I me. I grew up being a little troublemaker and a criminal when I was still a juvenile, but all that stopped when I moved here. It's just that my reputation followed me here. I graduated from high school and have a job delivering propane to ranches and houses outside the city. The only demon I have is my reputation.

"Have you been in trouble here?"

"No, but the sheriff, the tribal police, and Gallup Police Department have questioned me many times, primarily because of my only two friends. They're the criminals. He began to feel that he trusted Dolly and opened up to her.

"When I first moved here, the kids teased me because of my grandmother. They called her a witch, and a crazy woman, even though she's a tribal Shaman. But many rumors about my grandmother existed long before I came here."

"You've only had two friends all this time?"

Jimmy Running Water and Chris Leaping Bear were the only kids that didn't make fun of me. I call Jimmy 'Waste Water' because he's dirty. He fights dirty, and he steals from his people. Chris is not so bright and follows Jimmy like a trained dog. I call him 'Leaking Bear' because he acts like he pees his pants every time Jimmy gives him an order."

"Why do you hang around with boys like that?"

"I don't anymore. Things changed after high school. Jimmy and Chris have worsened, but I occasionally see them at Blackrock's. It's an old, abandoned house converted to a bar where everyone hangs out to party. I discovered that place when I first started delivering propane out there. I stay there sometimes when I'm in town. That's why I wanted to see Mr. Chile Charlie."

"I don't understand."

"I think they're the ones who broke into the museum."

"But the radio said nothing was taken," she reminded him.

"That's where everyone is wrong. Four rare Kachina masks were taken."

▲▲▲▲▲

Chris Leaping Bear drove alone into town in Jimmy's truck to get lunch back to Blackwater's. The Nearest Taco Bell was on Historical 60. After going through the drive-thru, Chris drove to gas up at a service station on the next block on the west end of the El Rancho Hotel front parking lot. He was about to leave when Nate came out of the hotel and walked toward Milly's truck. As Nate backed up to leave, Chris drove behind him and honked his horn to get his attention. Nate exited his vehicle, ready to deal with Jimmy again, but realized it was only Chris.

"Nate, hey, I'm sorry about all that with Jimmy. It's just that the buyer for the Kachina masks was here today, and we missed the meeting. That was $10,000 for each of us. That's why he was so angry. He thought you or your grandmother took the black sack we hid in the canyon."

"I didn't know anything about those masks until today," Nate told him.

"Anyway. I wanted to warn you about Strongbow. He's in this too and probably wants to talk to you."

"I know about Russell Strongbow. He's the one who asked me if I knew anyone for a job, but I didn't know what the job was going to be. He just told me I would receive a finder's fee." That note I gave Jimmy was from Strongbow."

"I thought you were the messenger."

"No, I just gave Jimmy a lead on a job. That's all."

## Chapter Sixteen

*Bad Day at Blackrock's*

Sam Blackrock sat behind the ill-constructed bar reading a magazine when Russell Strongbow bolted into the house like a raging grizzly bear.

"Where are they, Sam? He shouted.

Where's who?"

"Running Water and Leaping Bear, that's who!"

Chris isn't here, but Jimmy's in the back," Sam said, pointing to the hallway. "He's had a rough day already."

"It's gonna get a lot rougher," Strongbow said.

Strongbow kicked the door open and found Jimmy lying on a cot. He rushed towards Jimmy, lifted him by his shirt, and threw him against the wall. "Why didn't you show up at the meeting when you were supposed to?" He didn't give Jimmy a chance to answer. He grabbed him by the shirt again and pushed his face to the floor.

Jimmy was tough, but Strongbow was too powerful, too crazy, and too unpredictable. "Wait, Russ, I can explain!"

As Jimmy pushed himself up, Russell kicked his upper chest with a force that flipped Jimmy over on his back. "You're stealing the masks for yourselves, aren't you?"

"No! I'm telling you the truth. We weren't trying to steal them. Someone else stole them from us."

"What are you talking about?"

"We hid them in the canyon, and someone else dug them up when we returned."

"You expect me to believe a cheap lying thief like you?" Russell lifted Jimmy from the floor and was about to punch him.

"No! Wait! It's true. I think I know who has the masks. It's Nate Greystone and his grandmother."

"You mean Magi Milly?"

"Yes, we went to see her, and she knew we had been in the canyon. It had to be her and Greystone."

"I should have suspected that," Strongbow said, "Greystone's a lot smarter than you and Squatting Bear. Where's Greystone now?"

"He's on his way home. He came here to give us the message about the meet."

Russell notices the recent cut on Jimmy's face and the blunt haircut on the right side of his head. He realized the braided ponytail was gone. "He did that to you?"

Jimmy nodded. "Nate was angry because we went to see his grandmother."

"Did you search her house?"

"No."

Why not?"

Jimmy didn't respond.

Strongbow shook him. "Why Not!"

"She pulled a gun on us. That's why!"

Russell Strongbow chuckled. "Stay here. When your boyfriend, Stupid Bear, shows up, tell him to stay put and don't leave. Russell opened the left side of his brown leather vest to reveal a concealed handgun in a leather shoulder holster. "When I pull a gun, I use it." I'll be back later.

"Where are you going?" Jimmy asked.

"I'm not afraid of an old Medicine woman with a gun."

▲▲▲▲▲

Charlie took the Miyamura exit from I-40 and headed south towards the hotel to pick up Dolly. He stopped for the red light at Ford Drive and Historic 60. The El Rancho Hotel was located on the southwest corner of the intersection. He glanced at the hotel and saw Milly's truck in the parking lot facing west and another truck parked directly behind. Neither truck was parked in a parking stall.

The traffic light turned green, and Charlie decided to continue south on Ford Drive for a better view. He saw Nate talking with another man, and they seemed to be seriously discussing. Charlie continued south, turned left on Aztec Avenue, and immediately turned right onto the rear entrance of the hotel's east parking lot. He drove slowly up the parking lot, just far enough to get a distant view of the two boys. Something did not look right, Chile Charlie thought.

Dolly was about to watch TV when her cell phone rang.

"Dolly, we must go. Leave out the rear hotel entrance and wait for me by the street. Call me when you're there."

"Charlie, you're scaring me. What's going on?

"I'll explain when I pick you up. Hurry!" Charlie hung up intentionally to avoid further questions from Dolly. He kept an eye on Nate and the other man. He took out the note that Nate had left for his grandmother. It's the same notepad paper, and the writing looks the same, Charlie thought. His cell phone rang. It was Dolly.

"Charlie, I'm here now."

Charlie slowly backed his car, turned around, and exited the same entrance he drove into. He stopped on the road at the back of the hotel where Dolly waited. "Hurry, get in! Something's going on in the front of the hotel with Nate. He's talking to some guy," he explained.

Charlie drove north onto Navajo Drive and headed towards Historic 60, then turned right into the back of a convenience store at the west end of the hotel parking lot. He stopped. From there, he had a good view of the boys.

"Nate came into the hotel looking for you, Dolly told him. "He left the hotel some time ago. I didn't know he was still there,"

They watched Nate and the other man jumped into their trucks. Nate left the parking lot first, heading west on Historic 60. The other truck followed directly behind. As they passed by, Charlie and Dolly heard the roar of the second truck. Charlie backed up onto Navajo Drive and followed the trucks. He kept his distance so as not to be noticed.

"What's wrong, Charlie? You look serious?" she said.

"Greystone is involved in something, but I don't know for sure." He handed Dolly the blue note. "It's the same size, type, and color as the one I found in your room. And not only that, but I also recognized the sound of that truck following Nate. It's the same one I heard the night I searched your room and the one we heard that night in Tohatchi."

It suddenly dawned on Dolly. "Charlie!" she shouted.

"What?"

"Waste water! She said excitedly. "Nate told me that one of the boys he hangs around with is named Running Water. Nate calls him 'Waste Water.' The note was for his friend."

"Damn! That means Nate is involved." He paused. "You better call Gallup P.D. and get a hold of that Detective Trefren. Let him know what's going on, but don't mention anything about Kachina masks." Charlie paused. "That also means Nate knows who your boy is."

"What, Boy?" Dolly asked, surprised.

"You know . . . the one who attempted to rob you."

▲▲▲▲▲

Chile Charlie and Dolly followed the two trucks. Nate continued west, and Chris Leaping Bear turned south on Second Street. Charlie followed the loud truck.

"I think he's heading for a place called Blackrock's," Dolly said. "Nate said it was about seven miles south of Gallup."

Charlie continued south until the road changed to NM 602. He kept his distance. They had been out of the city for several miles and were now in open country of sage-covered hills. "Look, he's turning left onto that dirt road," he said.

The loud truck sped up, leaving a trail of dust. Charlie followed. He couldn't see the truck but could hear the noisy out-of-tune engine. He followed the dust trail for about a mile until it turned left onto a side road that sloped up a hill. Below the opposite side of the hill was a small valley of about five acres of flat desert land. A white stucco house stood in the center of the valley, hidden among the hills.

"That must be Blackrock's," Dolly said.

The noisy truck was parked in front of the house with no driver. Chris had walked into the house carrying a bag of tacos and a cardboard tray with two large soft drinks. As he entered the room, Jimmy jumped up from the cot.

"What took you so long? We gotta leave here now and hide somewhere as far as possible! Strongbow was here, and he thinks we stole the masks. I know he means to kill us."

"Where is he now?" Chris said, frightened.

"I told him about Nate and his grandmother. He's headed there now. If they have those Kachina masks Strongbow will find them."

"If he finds them, why do we have to hide?" Chris asked.

"Just in case he doesn't find them."

They rushed out of the room and headed for the front door. When they reached the porch, they saw Charlie standing next to Jimmy's truck and Dolly standing next to Charlie's car.

"So, you're the man with the El Camino. What are you doing here," Jimmy asked. He had previously seen Charlie's car in the hotel parking lot—a cream and turquoise 1959 El Camino was easy to spot anywhere.

"I'm here to ask a few questions. Are you Running Water?"

"Why do you want to know?"

"Because Nate Greystone is our friend, and I think he's involved in some kind of illegal activity with you two bums."

Jimmy walked down the porch steps towards his truck past Charlie. "I don't have time to answer questions, especially to a white man."

Charlie grabbed Jimmy by his coat, spun him around, and slammed him onto the driver's door. Dolly pulled open the front of her coat and revealed her holster with a revolver.

Chris dropped the tray of drinks. "Jimmy, she's got a gun!" he shouted.

"Make time, punk," Charlie said to Jimmy.

"I'll tell you what to want to know, mister!" Chris shouted. "Nate is our friend. We think he stole something from us."

"Like what, Kachina masks?" Charlie said.

The boys were stunned.

"Was Nate involved in that museum break-in?" Charlie asked.

"No, he had nothing to do with it," Chris said.

"Shut up, Chris! Jimmy shouted.

"I don't care about the museum. As far as anybody knows, nothing was taken. All you're responsible for is forced entry and putting a guard to sleep," Charlie explained.

Charlie looked over at Dolly.

She nodded. She recognized the man who attempted to rob her.

Charlie noticed an old scar on the left side of Jimmy's face. "By the way, Mr. Running Water, does my friend look familiar to you?"

Jimmy looked at Dolly and didn't respond.

"This is for Dolly," Charlie swung his right fist forward and slammed it into Jimmy's face. Jimmy's legs buckled, and his body slowly slid against the driver's door.

"Don't go anywhere," Charlie said to Chris. There's a man on his way here right now. His name is Detective John Trefren. He'll have questions for the both of you."

Charlie was about to walk away when he noticed a crumple blue notepad paper on the seat of Jimmy's truck. He reached through the opened window, took it out, and read it. He waved the blue note at Chris. "You don't mind if I take this, do you? He asked.

"No, take it," Chris said. "There's something you need to know. There's another man involved. His name is Russell Strongbow. He was here and roughed up Jimmy.

"He thinks Nate's grandmother might have those masks. He's *muy malo*, a bad man.

"So what?"

"He's gone to see Magi Milly . . . he'll kill her and Greystone.

▲▲▲▲▲

Charlie and Dolly headed to the Gallup police Department to speak with Detective Trefren. It was time to let him know everything. He was willing to go to jail for his part, and he was done with Blackrock and his two friends, who turned out not to be true friends.

Trefren was away from his office. He had been out investigating an armed robbery of a liquor store that had taken place the previous night. Nate decided to pick up his paycheck from the Arco Propane Company, get something to eat, then head home to speak with his grandmother. He planned to tell her about his involvement with Jimmy and Chris and the stolen and missing Sacred Kachina masks. As Shaman, she would be most interested to know.

## Chapter Seventeen

*Black Heart*

Nate placed his hand on his medicine bag as he drove home. It was time to take his culture seriously. The handle of the Bowie irritated his back, and he slipped it out from inside his belt and placed it beside him on the bench seat.

When he arrived home, he saw Strongbow's Dodge Ram parked before the Hogan. "What the hell is he doing here," Nate said. Maybe he wants me to give Jimmy another message, or he's looking for those two idiots. Nate noticed that Milly's horse was missing from the stable. He walked into the house and found it in complete disarray. The place had been ransacked. The table had been turned over, and everything in the dresser drawers and nightstands had been thrown on the floor.

"Surprised to find me here?" Russell Strongbow stood just outside the door.

"Why did you do this? You're looking for those masks, aren't you?"

"Where are they? Your friends seemed to think that you have them."

"They're not my friends anymore, and I don't have your masks. Where's my grandmother?'

"Tell me where the Kachina masks are, and I'll tell you where I have her hidden."

Anger rose in Greystone. "I told you; I don't have them, and if you've hurt my grandmother, I promise I will kill you."

Strongbow gave a fake laugh. "That seems to run in the family. But you won't kill me. Not when I have this." Strongbow pulls the .9mm Glock from his shoulder holster under his brown leather vest and points it at Nate's face.

Strongbow heard the approaching car. He instinctively turns his head. Nate grabs the gun and punches Strongbow in the face simultaneously. Strongbow attempts to loosen Nate's grip without success. He repeatedly hit Nate on the right side of his face until he released his grip. Strongbow's instinct was to shoot Nate, but not with a car approaching. He struck Nate's left side of the face with the side of the gun. Nate stumbles but still reaches to grab the gun. Three more strikes to the face with the side of the weapon, and Nate falls unconscious.

Charlie's El Camino comes to a sliding halt near the hogan. He rushes out of the car, and before he reaches the front door, Strongbow comes out of the Hogan, pointing his gun at Charlie.

"Stop right there! Strongbow shouted. "Put your hands up where I can see them."

"No, you drop the gun and put your hands up where I can see them," Dolly shouted.

When he rushed out of the door, Russel was so focused on dealing with Charlie that he failed to see Dolly standing behind him.

Strongbow looked to his left and saw a black woman pointing a .38 revolver directly at him. A flashing thought of Milly entered his mind. Had she summoned these demons to take me away? Reality came back. Federal Agents, he thought. Strongbow did not move or drop the gun. When he heard the hammer clicking as Dolly thumbed it back, he tossed his Glock to his right.

Charlie approached closer and bent over to pick up the gun. The force of Strongbow's kick on his upper chest flipped Charlie onto his back. The Glock flew out of his hands behind him. Strongbow dashed to pick it up, but Charlie rose, charged, and stuck Strongbow on his upper chest with his left shoulder and drove him back as if he was protecting the quarterback from a charging linebacker. They both crashed against the hogan. Charlie stepped back.

Dolly hesitated to shoot an unarmed man, but she resolved to shoot if the Strongbow was to pick up the gun.

The two men moved and weaved about, taking a measure of each other. They were of equal size, but Strongbow outweighed Chile Charlie with pure muscle and hatred. Strongbow whipped out his dagger from the sheath and lunged forward. Chile Charlie's hand met the descending blade with a claw-like grip of the wrist as his right fist crashed into Strongbow's face with all the power he could muster. The staggering blow took Strongbow by complete surprise. Before he could regain his balance, Chile Charlie drove another full-force punch into Strongbow's mouth as he held on to the wrist. The knife fell from Strongbow's hand.

Dazed and disarmed, Strongbow struck wildly and blindly. He had not expected this lanky man to hit so hard and quickly. Charlie continued to shoot stunning blows into Strongbow's bloody face. He knew he had gained the advantage and thought not to take risks. Both men paused, breathing hard, covered with blood from the splatter of the punches. Strongbow was blinded with blood and battered with a broken nose. He yielded ground, staggered back, then charged forward. Charlie swung his right fist, but Strongbow ducted and caught Charlie's left jaw with an agonizing right hook punch from the powerful man. Charlie fell back, dazed.

Strongbow turned and picked up his gun, but Charlie pounced on him like a mountain lion. The gun fired a single round as they struggled to control the weapon. Charlie heard a shrill cry. He saw Dolly drop to the ground but didn't see Strongbow's fist as it came down on his face. He staggered back, then saw the .9mm Glock pointed at him again.

"You'll die for this," Strongbow shouted through swollen lips. He lifted the gun to take careful aim at Charlie's head.

So, this is where it ends for Chile Charlie. He thought sadly, but not for himself. He was thinking about Dolly, lying lifeless in a pool of blood. With teary eyes, he looked squarely at the man about to take his life. The fire of the shot echoed loudly throughout the valley and instantly made Charlie's body flinch with a tremble.

Strongbow fell to his knees, bewildered. His left armed dangled with excruciating pain. The elbow bled. He looked up and saw the woman on a horse with a .45 revolver in her hand.

"Magi Milly," Strongbow said. He lifted his Glock to shoot the old woman."

The second shot went through his right thigh. Strongbow fell over, still holding on to his handgun.

"The third shot will be going right through your black heart, Russell Strongbow, and I will bury you in the desert where you will never be found," Milly warned.

The muscular man with the jewelry dropped the gun. Charlie was still as he watched this scene take place. It was surreal—like one of those western movies he loves to watch.

Charlie picked up Strongbow's gun and knife and ran over to Dolly. She moaned with pain. The .9mm bullet had struck her on the left leg through the femoral artery. Charlie removed his shirt, cut it with Strongbow's knife, and made a tourniquet to stop the bleeding. Milly went inside the Hogan, where Greystone was lying on the floor, bleeding from the face but conscious.

Charlie noticed the CB antenna on the Dodge Ram. He called for help on the emergency channel and requested medical assistance for two shooting victims and an injured victim. He carried Dolly onto Milly's bed. With reluctance, he attended to Strongbow's injuries and stabilized him until the ambulance arrived. Charlie left him on the ground, agonized by his bullet wounds.

▲▲▲▲▲

John Trefren arrived shortly in his unmarked police car, lights flashing and siren blaring. He jumped out of his car with a gun as he assessed the crime scene. He saw Charlie come out of the hogan.

"How did you get here so soon," Charlie asked.

"Chris leaping Bear told me there would be trouble here. I was just a few miles away when the emergency call came out on the police radio." Trefren smiled. The Calvary is on its way."

Within the hour, many emergency units were on the scene—the tribal police, sheriff's department, fire department, ambulances, two medical helicopters, and the FBI.

Strongbow was flown out in one medical helicopter, handcuffed to the gurney. Dolly was flown in the other medical chopper, and Greystone was transported by ambulance. Everyone was taken to Gallup Indian Medical Center, where Dolly underwent immediate surgery. It was late evening when all the police investigations, scene processing, and interviews were concluded.

Charlie headed for the hospital to see Dolly. The hospital receptionist informed him that Dolly was recovering in ICU.

Dolly was asleep, connected to monitors and IV. The attending nurse checked her vitals. "You can come in for a moment. She's resting," the nurse said.

"Dolly, it's me, Chile Charlie," he whispered. His eyes welled, but he fought back the tears.

She opened her eyes slightly. "Chile Charlie," She smiled.

Charlie clutched her hand and kissed her forehead. He pulled up a chair next to her bed, "I'm sorry, Dolly. I never meant for you to get involved in all this." He shook his head. "And I surely didn't expect that you would get shot." His lips quivered.

Dolly was still drowsy from her surgery. "It wasn't your fault Charlie," she said in a slow hushed voice with eyes closed. "I was the one who got you involved in all this. I just happened to be at the wrong place at the right time. It was an accident," Dolly said as she barely opened her eyes. "Remember, I'm from the projects of North Chicago." Dolly closed her eyes and went into a deep slumber.

▲▲▲▲▲

Nate Greystone was released from the hospital on the same evening with a mild concussion and bruises on his face. Charlie drove him back home and took the opportunity to find out what he needed to know.

"Greystone, how did you get involved in all this in the first place?"

"I wasn't involved at all. It started the day I was filling the propane tank behind the Native

American Museum when Russell Strongbow came out the back door and asked me if I knew a couple of men who would do a job for him. He said it was a business deal that would pay $10,000 per person, and I would get a 'finder's fee' out of it. I knew it was going to be something terrible.

"I guess Strongbow worked at the museum, but his brown Dodge Ram was parked in the back as if he tried to hide, which I thought was weird. He went to his car, returned with a small notepad, and wrote down his cell number. He told me to give the note to my contact. Then he ripped off half of the notepad from the sticky part and gave it to me. He said not to use phones for communication, just the notepad."

"Was it a blue notebook? Charlie asked.

"Yeah. How did you know?" Greystone asked, surprised.

"Because I found one you wrote in Dolly's room at the El Rancho Hotel the night someone tried to rob her."

"I didn't know anything about that. I swear," Nate said apologetically. "Strongbow called me with the message. I wrote it down to give to Jimmy

Running Water. That was the night before I met you and Dolly."

Charlie liked Greystone, but he would not forgive him if he had taken part in the attempted robbery at the hotel. He needed to know the extent of Greystone's involvement. "Were you with Jimmy and Chris that night?"

"No, I was gambling at Blackstone's, trying to regain my losses."

Charlie thought for a moment. That explains the whistle I heard outside that night, Chris must have been waiting somewhere in the parking lot, and Jimmy whistled to get his attention to pick him up.

"What about the Perea note?"

"I didn't write that one. Russell Strongbow called me and told me he had a note for me to give to Jimmy. I met him at the airport but couldn't find Jimmy until later. I knew nothing about Kachina masks until Jimmy and Chris accused me of stealing them. Someone took those masks, and Jimmy was mad. I hear he didn't meet with the buyer, and everybody lost half a million on the money. That's why Strongbow wanted to kill everyone."

"So, who is Li?"

"All I know is that he drives a white SUV and met with Jimmy in Tohatchi one night."

"And that information came from Strongbow when he called you, right?"

"Yeah."

Charlie felt relieved to learn Greystone was not involved directly in either crime. "You'll have to report all this to the police, you know," Charlie told him.

## Chapter Eighteen

*Gift of the Spirits*

Detective John Trefren was sitting at his desk reading over the police investigation reports when Chile Charlie walked into his office with Nate Greystone trailing behind.

"How's the investigation going, Detective?" Charlie asked.

Trefren shook his head with frustration. "Nobody's talking. So far, we have two unidentified men tying up the security guard, entering the museum, and didn't take anything. We know they were looking for something because they left a mess in the inventory room."

"You have any evidence?" Charlie asked.

"Not much. They must've been wearing gloves. All we found were a few strands of hair."

Charlie smiled at Trefren. "This is your lucky day, detective. Nate here has a story for you."

Nate told the detective about his detached involvement regarding the break-in and Jimmy,

Chris, and Russell Strongbow but did not mention masks.

"It'll be your word against theirs, and the rest is hearsay. We have no proof they were the break-in's culprits," Trefren said.

Charlie retrieved a blue notepad and the two crumbled notes from his coat pocket and placed them on Trefren's desk. "This is the notepad that Strongbow ripped out of his notepad and gave to Nate. You'll find that the rips match the other half of the notepad in Strongbow's Dodge Ram. You can still see the imprint on the top sheet where Strongbow wrote his phone number. Nate wrote only one note, and he wrote it on the bottom sheet of the pad." Charlie points to one of the notes. "This is the one written by Nate. Strongbow wrote the other one."

Trefren read and compared the two notes. "Russell Strongbow and I have been close friends since we were young. I've always known he was bad medicine," he said with sadness.

"I'm sorry to hear that," Charlie said. "If you check the phone records, you'll find that Strongbow made those phone calls to Nate, " he reported. All the other pieces fall in place."

Nate Greystone reached into his medicine bag. "Here's your proof," he said as he placed the braided ponytail on the desk. "DNA. It was a gift from Running Water." You'll find that he was in the inventory room that night.

Detective Trefren smiled and put the evidence in a plastic bag. "I don't understand why Russell wanted to meet with Jimmy at Perea."

Charlie and Nate looked at each other, then at Trefren, and shrugged without a word.

"That leaves me with one question, who is Li?" Trefren said.

"Strongbow and Jimmy, they're the only two who know," Greystone blurted.

The room went silent.

"Three," Chile Charlie said. "I know who he is."

▲▲▲▲▲

Detective Trefren entered the Native American Museum with five patrol officers. He informed the female receptionist that he was there to see the museum director.

"What is this about," she asked with a frightened look.

"Tell him, private business," Trefren responded.

She entered the director's office, closed the door behind her, and returned almost immediately.

"Mr. Acothley will see you now," she said, pointing to the door. She returned to her desk and picked up the phone.

"What can I do for you, gentleman? The director said as he stood up from his desk.

"Are you Leon Acothley, and is that your white Kia SUV parked out front," Trefren asked.

"Yes, I am, and that is my car."

Mr. Acothley had a sober look on his face. He was an older man with black rim glasses, short hair, gray hair, and light skin, more white man than

Native American. He wore western attire and an over-kill of turquoise and silver jewelry, much like Russell Strongbow — perhaps to show his link to his Navajo ancestry.

"Mr. Acothley, are you familiar with a Russell Strongbow? Trefren asked.

"Why yes, the gentleman works for me."

"What exactly does he do for you?"

"He's part of the intake staff. They're responsible for obtaining and cataloging all the museum's items," Leon Acothley answered.

"Do you know a Jimmy Running Water?"

"Ah, no, no, I'm not familiar with that person," Acothley said, appearing nervous.

"Then who was that person who parked next to your KIA that night at the Tohatchi Chapter House? Trefren didn't wait for an answer. "Leon Acothley, I'm arresting you for Conspiracy of Theft of Native American artifacts."

"This must be a mistake," Acothley responded.

Detective Trefren maintained a professional police demeanor. "Sir, I have two witnesses who will testify that you were the head of the conspiracy and hired them to break into the museum to steal items for the black market."

"But nothing was taken from this museum. I didn't steal anything, and my attorney is on his way here now!" Acothley rambled in nervous confusion.

"First of all, Mr. Acothley, you're not being charged with theft, just conspiracy, and second, why did you have your receptionist call your attorney if you're innocent?"

Leon Acothley was placed into custody and escorted out of the museum by two Gallop police patrol officers.

▲▲▲▲▲

Detective John Trefren had arrested Jimmy Running Water and Chris Leaping Bear at Blackrock's and charged them with Attempted Robbery. The Sheriff's Department arrested Sam Blackrock for operating a gambling house, various liquor violations, using a house of prostitution, and contributing to the delinquency of minor girls. Several others were also arrested—mostly underage patrons and the ladies of the house. Several weeks later, the county condemned the house, and Blackrock's was no more.

The interrogations of the two boys went moderately well. They both claimed they went to the museum, but after searching the place, they found nothing worth taking. Chris was more cooperative and corroborated Nate's report after he was threatened with charges of kidnapping on top of burglary and attempted robbery. Chris accepted a deal, and all the charges against him were dropped, except for burglary. Jimmy Running Water was not so fortunate. On top of the other crimes, he was also charged with felony menacing and attempted murder. Neither Jimmy nor Chris ever mentioned Kachina masks.

## Chapter Nineteen

### *Ceremony*

Two days after Dolly was released from the hospital, she and Chile Charlie drove to Milly's hogan in mid-morning.

"So why are we going up to Milly's again?" Dolly asked.

"I don't know. Greystone called me, and he said that she wanted to tell us something important but didn't say what," Charlie explained. "Anyway, leaving that hotel room for fresh air will be good."

As they drove on the red dirt road, about a mile away from Milly's hogan, they saw several clouds of smoke rising from the direction of the house. When they neared, they saw many cars, pickup trucks, and motorcycles parked along both sides of the road leading up to the Hogan.

Dolly's heartbeat increased as they got closer. "God, I hope everything is all right," she said. Maybe something has happened to Milly, she thought.

There were crowds of people — men, women, children — in colorful ceremonial clothing. When they exited the car, they heard the loud pounding of drums and the chanting of songs. Behind the hogan were several bond fires and people dancing in circular directions around the fires.

Charlie took a folded wheelchair from the back of his car and helped Dolly into it. He pushed her towards the house, then two young Navajo boys stood in front and blocked his path. One boy signaled that he would push Dolly's wheelchair.

Milly sat in her chair among a line of elderly men and women. She stood up, raised both arms and wide, holding her staff in one hand. The music and singing stopped.

"Welcome, Chile Charlie and Dolly," Magi Milly said. "These are reverent men and women. They are the Shaman, the Singers, and the Medicine people from the many tribes that make up our nation. They, and all these people, have come from distant places to honor you today."

Charlie didn't know what to say. There were so many people there. "Honor me for what," he asked.

"Chile Charlie, you have saved an ancient tradition of our people. You found the sacred Kachina masks of the ancient spirits and returned them to the Navajo. These people are here to praise you and sing songs of your journey as a way of thanks," Milly said.

Dolly reached for his hand and held it tightly. She was very proud of Charlie.

Milly sat down, and the drums and chants resumed. The people sang in perfect harmony in their colorful attire, jewelry, and feathered headbands.

"Come, Charlie, join us in dance and food. This is your day," Greystone said. He directed Charlie to a semi-circle of men sitting on the grassy ground—they looked more like warriors. Chile Charlie sat on the ground with his legs crossed, and Greystone sat beside him. Charlie noticed that Detective John Trefren sat among the semicircle of warriors.

Dolly was ushered to the other side of the ceremonial circle. A ceremonial headband was placed on her head, and women lined up on each side of her wheelchair and danced in place.

Large wool blankets were placed in front of Charlie by elderly women. A young girl approached Charlie and put a feathered headband as the other men wore on his head. People began to enter the semi-circle with gifts for their honored guests. An older woman placed a wool blanket on Charlie's back and draped it around his shoulders. Greystone rose and approached Milly. The music stopped again. Charlie couldn't make out what they were doing. Greystone turned and returned to the warriors' circle, and Milly followed. The music started, but this time with a slower beat of the drums and a somber chant.

Greystone enters the semi-circle with his palms up, carrying something wrapped in a red cloth. He approached Charlie with slow ceremonial movements. "Chile Charlie, this is a gift from Magi Milly and me." He unwrapped the cloth and extended his arms to Charlie. It was his Greystone's Bowie Knife.

"Greystone, that's your knife. Your grandfather gave it to you. It's been in your family for generations," Charlie told him. "I can't accept that. This should stay in your family,"

"It *is* in the family," Milly said. "You are family now. Take it with you so you will always remember the way of the Navajo."

Charlie's throat tightened, and his eyes began to well. Dolly was not as strong as Charlie. Her tears ran unabated.

By late afternoon, the blankets were covered with gifts made by the people, blankets, jewelry, dreamcatchers, Kachina dolls, wood carvings, and one horse saddle.

Trefren stood before Charlie and squatted in front of him. "Tell me, Charlie, how did you figure out Leon Acothley was behind the break-in?"

"That's easy. Strongbow worked at the museum and parked his car behind the building as if he were hiding. He didn't strike me as one who categorizes valuable artifacts. Who else would allow Strongbow to go in and out of the museum as if he owned the place? Director *Lee*-on Acoth-*lee*," he said, pronouncing each syllable slowly with an emphasis on *Lee*.

"Charlie, you have the investigator spirit in you. By the way, this whole thing about ancient

Kachina masks, it's just a myth, okay?" Trefren said as he nodded.

"You don't believe in them?" Charlie asked, surprised.

Trefren chuckled. "What do you think, Mr. Investigator? I'm Navajo."

▲▲▲▲▲

The sun began to set, and Charlie watched as Milly stood at the edge of a shallow cliff behind the hogan. Like sunrises, she loved to watch the sunsets as well. Charlie walked up and stood next to her.

"Look at the color of the desert," Milly said. "See how it changes?" She paused. "In your journey, what did you learn, Chile Charlie?"

"I learned that the spirit of my dead wife and my family will always be with me. Bodies come and go, but the spirits will always be here with us."

"As with the spirit of the earth," Milly said.

Charlie's investigative curiosity overwhelmed him. He had to ask. "Milly, what happened to the Kachina masks? The day I came to see you, I left the black sack in your hogan when you went to the stables."

"The masks have returned to the desert where the Kachina spirits left them. The desert keeps its secrets and will only reveal them when ready. Mother Earth provided you with drink, food, and shelter. The desert sent the coyote and eagle spirits to direct you to the sacred masks to take and protect them. You are a good man, and the Spirits will always watch over you, Chile Charlie."

Charlie smiled and cast his eyes toward the colorful sunset. It was Milly. She had just returned from the desert when she shot Russell Strongbow. The medicine woman, Magi Milly, set out on horseback on an early winter day, returned the sacred Kachina masks to the desert, and hid them in a secret place like that body—never to be found.

## THE END

# ADVENTURE TWO

## NAVAJO REVENGE

## CHAPTER ONE

### *The Chapel*

"I have heard there is a Chapel in the village of Chimayó that has a back room filled with healing dirt, and I would like to check it out," Dolly informed Chile Charlie.

"It would please me greatly if you said yes."

Charlie smiled, pulled his railroader's pocket watch out of his shirt, looked, and said, "Of course, we have plenty of daylight left. We can make it a side trip. Let's do it."

They arrived at Chimayó, much to their pleasure, after a hair-raising, hour-long drive on the narrow, twisting country back road. Charlie had to drive slowly and super cautiously.

This historic village, a tight-knit community of 3,000 people, was established by Spanish settlers at the tail-end of the 17th century.

Some buildings looked like they may have been built then. They had the mystic of old age.

Charlie drove directly to the Chimayó Chamber of Commerce office. Once inside, Dolly picked up a colorful brochure and asked Charlie, "Would you like me to read what I found?"

"Yes, go ahead. I want to learn about the Chapel."

Dolly reads, "Chimayó is known internationally for its Catholic Chapel, the El Santuario de Chimayò. The Chapel was built to mirror the splendor of Mexico and Spain's architecture."

Dolly leaned close to Charlie's shoulder and said, "Look, here is a picture of the Chapel. What do you think? Does the Chapel look like what you thought it would?

"No, but it doesn't matter," Charlie said.

Dolly continued reading, "A private individual built the Chapel in 1816 so local people could worship Jesus. Then in 1929, preservationists bought it and bequeathed it to the Archdiocese of Santa Fe.

The Chapel has a reputation as a healing site. The believers claim the dirt from the Chapel's backroom would heal physical and spiritual ills. A fable is that a person may take one handful of the healing dirt because God will replace it. The dirt will never expire.

The Chapel became known as the "Lourdes of America" and attracted 300,000 visitors yearly. There have been writers who have called it the most important Catholic pilgrimage center in the United States. In 1970 the sanctuary was designated as a national historic landmark."

Dolly put the brochure down. She turned to Charlie and smiled, "Shall we get some dirt to soothe our physical and mental ills," Dolly asked?

Charlie said, "Yes, but I thought Chimayò was known for the weaving traditions of the Ortega and Trujillo families. They have weaved in the Spanish colonial tradition for generations. The family's traditional crafts include tin smithing, wood carving, and making religious paintings. Families have practiced those crafts in the region for years. These activities, along with the local architecture and the landscape of irrigated fields, create a historical ambiance that attracts many visitors each year."

"Yes, that is right, the village is also known for its heirloom Chile Peppers. In 2003, the Native Hispanic Institute's founder Marie Pilar Compos wrote the Chimayó Chile Project. Her book revived the 300-year-old native seed stock business," Dolly said. The local restaurants use them to enhance the flavor of popular Mexican foods.

## CHAPTER TWO

*Strange behavior*

The drive from Chimayó to Gallup was pleasant and uneventful. The sky took on a beautiful orange color as the sunset. Chile Charlie looked at his pocket watch—6:45--dinnertime.

Neither Dolly Sweet Thompson nor Chile Charlie wanted to eat. He grabbed his and Dolly's overnight bag from the back of his El Camino. They walked side by side into the El Rancho Hotel lobby and directly to their rooms.

As Chile Charlie handed Dolly her bag, he said, "Thanks for the exciting adventure, Dolly. You were great, get some rest, and I will see you tomorrow."

He inserted the key and disappeared into his room.

Dolly stood for a moment, dumbfounded by Charlie's quick disappearing act.

Chile Charlie ensured that his room thermostat was set at 65, which experts determined is the best for human sleeping temperature. He removed his shoes and slipped out his jacket, shirt, and pants to prepare him for a nap.

Charlie woke up with a start and remembered he had not showered. He walked into the shower stall, set the water temperature to medium-hot, and showered.

# CHAPTER THREE

### *Crimewave*

Charlie woke up after a restful night and prepared himself for his new day, including a cup of in-room coffee.

There came a knock on the door; Charlie looked out the window to see who was there. He unlatched and opened the door. Henry Goodlad burst into the room and asked, "How in the heck can we stop this crime wave that has hit our community?"

"How should I know, Henry? I don't live here. I live in Las Cruces," Chile Charlie answered.

Henry Goodlad was a short, round-faced man with a barrel chest characteristic of a Navajo blood mixture.

Henry poured coffee into a plastic container sitting idle beside the coffee pot and sipped it. Then he got a donut and took a large bite. Chewing vigorously, Henry continued his description of last night's happening.

"Last night, there was a fight downtown where a Navajo was cut up badly. A drunken Mexican did it. The Navajo didn't die, but he will not be up and around for a while," Goodlad told Charlie.

"Doesn't Gallup have a reputation for crime and violence," Chile Charlie asked. "The railroad, Interstate Highway, and mixed culture may contribute to the problem.

I read a study by Brad Zukerman of the University of Oregon that indicated the relationship between Interstate highways, railroads, and criminal activity is available but vague and scarcely researched. Voices on both sides of the debate frequently reference claims to one end or another, despite little empirical evidence in the field supporting their claims. I found the same scant evidence about mixed cultures.

# CHAPTER FOUR

*Zodiac Sign*

Born January 15, Chile Charlie's Zodiac sign is Capricorn. He thought of himself as a planner extraordinaire. He plans his actions to the last minute; that's what he thinks. His plans sometimes work out differently than he wants them to. He is not a planner on paper. His planning is always in his mind.

At six o'clock in the morning the following day, Chile Charlie pulled his two-inch red suspenders over his shoulders, exiting out the door of his room with a blast of energy. He slid into the driver's side of his trusty El Camino, buckled the seat belt, started the engine, put the truck in reverse, and backed into the street. He wanted to look at the city parks that have received attention in the New Mexico Magazine.

# CHAPTER FIVE

## *The body*

Chile Charlie and Dolly Sweet Thompson were finishing their bacon and eggs breakfast when they heard a radio news report. There was a body found three blocks away from the El Rancho Hotel. The victim's description made Dolly think that the same person had tried to enter her room before.

She encouraged Chile Charlie to join her in checking the crime scene for identification. "Will you take me to see the body," Dolly asked.

"OK, if that will make you happy," Charlie answered.

Arriving at the crime scene, they found the body lying face down, the neck nearly severed, and legs set apart about afoot. The hands crossed the victim's back as if they were being readied to be tied.

Detective Red Shoe said, "The body was found by a local businessman on his way to open his store. It was soaked from an unusual thunderstorm that moved through last night. Not that it mattered much."

A second Gallup detective explained, "No identification of the person was found, but we might be able to identify the body using facial recognition techniques."

Detective Red Shoe said, "He was an unlucky vagrant common in Gallup—the murder capital of New Mexico, as was reported in the Albuquerque Journal."

Dolly asked the detective to turn the body over so she could see the face. Upon doing so, Dolly's face turned to horror. She cried and told the detective that the body was the same person who had broken into my room.

Fifteen minutes later, two additional patrol officers and three ambulance crew members arrived.

Chile Charlie saw the street was stained with the blood of the murdered victim. He turned away to see Dolly's reaction. Her reaction was stoic. But Charlie felt Dolly was wondering why.

Red Shoe decided it would be best to proceed as if a crime had been committed, and they prohibited the ambulance crew from approaching the scene. Then another detective arrived, then another. They searched the area and found nothing helpful.

One officer took photographs and videoed the body. They studied the tracks around the street and found no useable evidence.

The third officer came back from his radio car and reported the identification that the body belonged to Red Deer of the Hopi Crown Point Clan. "This information may help solve the killing," said the officer.

Another officer took Charlie aside and wondered why he and Dolly were at the crime scene.

Charlie told the officer about the break-in events the previous day.

Later, Chile Charlie and Dolly Thompson met for lunch at the El Rancho Hotel restaurant. Charlie turned his attention to his coffee cup and took a sip. It was cold. He asked the waiter for a warm-up.

# CHAPTER SIX

## *Discovery*

They arrived in Gallup in time for dinner but were not ready to eat. The afternoon lunch was still heavy on their bellies.

"Let's take a nap and eat later," questioned Dolly.

"That sounds like a plan," said Charlie.

Dolly Thompson was not devoid of sexual experiences in Chicago. She wondered whether Chile Charlie's sexual drive was a buckaroo cowboy or an inquisitive kitty cat. She was conniving to determine how she would discover.

As they neared Gallup, Chile Charlie opened the conversation by saying, "Dolly, how about a cup of tea as a nightcap after this hectic day?"

Dolly saw her opening to get Charlie alone. She said, No, but I have some cold beer in the hotel refrigerator, and I would share a bottle with you."

Charlie thought momentarily, then he announced, "Dolly, that sounds like a great idea. A cold beer right now would go down nicely."

Dolly reached over and hugged Charlie with great tenderness. This action surprised Charlie beyond words.

Dolly said, "Charlie, do you not like me that way?"

'What way is that, Dolly, asked Charlie.

"You know. As she moved his right hand to her belly that way," she whispered.

"I didn't know you had any romantic interest in a person like me, Dolly, and I'm not sure I can still get it up anyway. It has been such a long time," said Charlie.

"Maybe we should try it to make sure," said Dolly, suggesting they retire to her room.

As Chile Charlie and Dolly Thompson entered her room, Dolly shed her dress and underwear.

Charlie was hesitant about removing his clothes. He feared Dolly might have laughed at him because he was a string bean and stature. He did not have an atlas-looking physique.

"Don't be silly, Charlie," said Dolly. You know I like you for your authentic self. Let me help you with those clothes.

Dolly helped Charlie get out of his suspenders and pants, and he removed his shirt. Then she slipped his shorts below his knees and steadied him as he got them off his feet. Leading him to the bed, Dolly said, now you get in first and lie down on your back while I amuse myself for a little bit.

Though foreplay was about to begin, Dolly moved beside him, and they kissed passionately as Dolly gently massaged Charlie's relaxed parts. She put her left nipple in his mouth and watched his tone be erected membrane. She pushed his finger into her wet vagina and increased the pace of her manipulation. Then she leaned over to practice her cheek-to-cheek arts.

Dolly climbed aboard and enveloped Charlie's swollen organ. Slowly, she thrust her pelvis into his direction, savoring all the attendant sensations. The crescendo coincided, timing her movements and excitement to coincide with her partner's progress.

After a few minutes, Dolly lifted herself from Charlie's chest and, looking at him, said, "Well,

Charlie, I guess you're not ready for the grave just yet!"

"You're not a buckaroo or a kitty cat but a wonderful lover," stated Dolly.

Greatly satisfied with her accomplishments, Dolly rested her head on a pillow and drifted to dreamland.

# CHAPTER SEVEN

*A second body was found.*

As Chile Charlie and Dolly arrived at the restaurant, the radio announcer said, "A second body of a male Navajo man was found in almost the exact place as the first murder victim found several days ago."

Dolly said, "Let's go see it."

Chile Charlie was not in the mood to look at a dead body. He wanted to eat but reluctantly agreed to tag long.

When they arrived at the location of the body, they saw the dead body lying on its back, the legs slightly parted, the right arm at his side, and the left hand across the chest with the wrist and hand extending oddly rigid.

The dead Navajo's hair was braided but not in long braids. The dead man had a white man's haircut.
He had been in knife fights that scared and disfigured his would-have-been handsome face.

This man, the detective said, cut up another Mexican in Gallup. He was a drunk, conjecture of the detective. The dead person was identified as Edwardo Yellow Skin. He belonged to the **Tohatchi Clan.** His rap sheet was a mile long.

It included three arrest reports for being drunk and disorderly, assault and battery incidences, and driving while under the influence of alcohol charges. The last entry was an account of the knifing in a Gallup bar and a car stolen and abandoned after the knifing.

Chile Charlie and Dolly wondered if there was any connection between the two killings. Both Navajos were found in the street without an apparent reason for their murder.

Chile Charlie thought it would be extremely complicated to make any connections.

Chile Charlie turned to Dolly and began, "In 1974, there was a great deal of turmoil in Gallup regarding the treatment of the members of the Navajo Nation. It was like an evil spirit drifting down from the sandpaper mesas and scrub-pickled hillsides.

That year the bodies of three Navajo men were found in a nearby canyon, burned, and bludgeoned. The three white high school students killed the two Navajo men. The students were sent to prison and reform school.

The violence and mild sentences incited marches by Navajos through Gallup's streets and exposed tensions between them and the town's predominantly white residents."

The United States Commission on Civil Rights eventually investigated and found widespread mistreatment and prejudice against Navajos.

There were two mysterious killings of Navajo men, thought Dolly. Was there any connection between the incidence of forty years ago and today's deaths? Dolly raised the question to Detective Red Shoe.

He eyed Dolly and yelled, "Are you crazy?"

"How could something that happened so long ago be connected? Get Real."

Dolly was taken aback by Red Shoe's outbreak; she placed her hands on her broad hips and shouted, "No! I am not crazy; I know long-lived hatred may still exist. They do not just die away like moths in the night."

Charlie came to Dolly's rescue, saying he read that six days after the boys were sent off to prison, a Navajo man killed a white Gallup police officer.

There was a struggle in a Wal-Mart parking lot, the police report read.

The Navajo said the police officer assaulted his girlfriend. The Navajo attacked the officer by grabbing his baton and aggressively beating the police officer to death. The police report stated that this Navajo man had a history of violence.

Detective Red Shoe turned on Chile Charlie as a man who had lost control of his emotions yelled, "That has nothing, I mean nothing, to do with the dead man before us now. Get off the history lecture.

Dolly turned to Charlie, and with a flick of her eyebrows, she said it was time for us to get out of here.

Charlie gave an agreeing nod. And away they went.

Fifteen minutes later, they arrived at the hotel restaurant. They asked for a table for two in a quiet corner. After seated, Charlie asked Dolly what she thought about Detective Red Shoe's emotional outburst.

"He was very defensive," mumbled Dolly.

"That was my feeling too; I wondered why," answered Charlie.

The waiter came by just as Charlie finished his query. The waiter wanted to know if he could take their order. Charlie said plainly, "Not yet; we have yet to have a chance to look over the menu.

"But please bring us some hot coffee along with cream and sugar. We will make up our minds soon; thank you," Chile Charlie announced authoritatively.

"Well, Dolly, what on the menu looks good to you?

"My treat tonight," stated Chile Charlie, thinking he would impress her.

"The lobster looks good to me, but it is not fresh, probably flown in frozen, so I'll go with the Green Enchilada with an egg over the top.

Charlie let out the breath he was holding because he was not sure he had the funds to cover the cost of lobster. Thank God for small favors, he thought.

The waiter returned with their coffee, and they placed their exact order of Green Enchiladas with an egg over the top.

Both Dolly and Charlie leaned back and slowly sipped their hot coffee. They retreated into their dreamland of thoughts. Neither said a word as they took deep-satisfying sips of coffee, lost in study. Seconds flew by into short minutes.

Dolly asked Charlie, "Do you think there are any religious overtones in those murderers?"

"Dolly, that's a fascinating question; I haven't thought of that until now," Charlie said.

"Let's think back. What was the day of the week of your arrival in Gallup? Do you remember?

"Sunday, of course," Dolly quipped.

"Do you think the day of the week would make any difference?

"No, but a little research might be in order," Charlie responded.

There came a swishing sound--like a gust of air. A large platter came with two picture-perfect magazine plates of Green Enchilada with an egg on top.

"Whoa, look at that, Dolly! Are you ready for this feast or not?

"You got to be kidding. I am starved and will have no problem with this meal, and I can assure you, Charlie," Dolly exclaimed.

As they each took their first bite, there was a collective *ahhhhhh,* this is good, and I mean good! They continued eating silently, punctuated with a pleasing smile, "I like this!"

After their meal, they each order a second cup of black coffee.

"Now, Dolly, your question was, is there a connection between the murders?" Right?

"Yes, there is, but I sure don't know what it could be right now," offered Charlie.

Dolly faced Charlie head-on with a questioning statement, "Are you as tired as I am? Let's take a nap. We will be fresh-eyed after."

Charlie agreed to nap, and they went to their separate rooms.

As Charlie tried to nap, his mind returned to his conversation with Blue Rope regarding revenge.

He could not get Navajo revenge is personal, Is Personal, Is personal.

## CHAPTER EIGHT

*A hunch*

Chile Charlie awoke from his nap with an idea buzzing in his mind. He was eager to act on his hunch. First, he had to wake up Dolly.

Charlie showered, brushed his teeth, and dressed. He stepped into the hallway and knocked briskly on Dolly's door. While waiting for her to answer, Charlie paced to deduce his excessive energy.

Dolly called out, "Who's there?

"It's me. Get dressed and meet me in the restaurant as fast as possible," Chile Charlie answered.

"OK, I'll be there as fast as I can, but you know, I had a wonderful dream when you knocked, whispered Dolly.

Dolly joined Charlie and ordered black coffee and an English muffin with peanut butter twenty minutes later. She was full of life after a two-hour nap. The world would be her oyster, and she felt it.

Charlie had his third cup of coffee and was high-spirited. But he thought it would be the right thing to do to order breakfast. He ordered French toast.

As they ate, Charlie told Dolly, "I think, just maybe, there is a way to solve the two killings here. Are you game to give my hunch a try?"

"I am not sure. What do we have to do," asked Dolly.

"We will head out for Navajo Nation's Tribal Headquarters in Window Rock, Arizona," Charlie quipped.

"I just don't see why a trip to Arizona will help solve this mystery in New Mexico," Dolly said.

"Dolly, when I took Blue Rope aside, he told me about the Ghost Dance and, more importantly, the code of Navajo revenge. There could be a linkage. Baby me," Charlie explained.

"OK, let's give it a try. I will pack for three days and meet you at the El Camino in an hour," replied Dolly.

# CHAPTER NINE

## *Early hostilities*

Chile Charlie was reminded of Jean-Baptiste Alphonse Karr's 1849 famous quotation, "The more things change, and the more they stay the same."

"Do you think all the present-day emphasis on social media would cause the Navajos to change their traditional beliefs regarding revenge," Charlie asked.

Dolly needed help figuring out how to respond to Charlie's question. She changed the discussion.

Dolly stated, "Charlie, I will tell you the story of two men-- both named Narbona, although not related to each other-- and how the canyon pass came to be named after one of them."

"Around the 1400s, the Navajo tribes were nomadic hunters and gatherers who migrated into the Four Corners Region. They were thought to be cousins to Eskimos.

Individual civilians and Navajos could be victims of conflicts and instigate conflicts to serve their interests. Hostilities escalated between

European Americans and the Navajos following the respected Navajo leader Narbona's death.

Colonel Edwin Summers established Fort Defiance near present-day Window Rock for the United States government. This event was before the Long Walk and the treaties signed in 1849, 1858, and 1861.

In 1804, a Navajo tribe raided the Spanish outpost north of Laguna Pueblo. The area was in the shadow of Mount Taylor. It was a sacred Navajo mountain. Losing their holy place to the Spanish was harsh. The tribe wanted the land returned for grazing and survival.

Typical truces and treaties said the army would protect the Navajo tribes. However, the military allowed other Native American tribes and Mexicans to steal livestock and capture Navajo as enslaved people."

"A truce between the army and Navajo tribes was signed on February 15, 1861. The Navajos tribes were again promised protection, but as part of the truce, two of the Navajo's four sacred mountains and about one-third of their traditionally held land were taken from them. In March 1861, a company of fifty-two citizens led by Jose Manuel Sanchez drove off Navajo horses. Still, Captain Wingate followed the trail and recovered the horses for the Navajo tribes. But the Navajos killed Sanchez for an unknown reason."

"Another group of European settlers ravaged Navajo Rancherias near Beautiful Mountain. Rancheria was a Spanish term for small Indian settlements. The Rancherias were developed from small Navajo groups on the outskirts of American settlements. These groups were fleeing or avoiding removal to a reservation."

"One day, a party of Mexicans and Pueblo Indians captured 12 Navajos in a raid, and three were brought in. Lieutenant Colonel Antonio Narbona retaliated with a contingency of Spanish soldiers. They used the pass to enter Canyon de Chelly. The Navajo tribes were severely defeated. This action caused a time of fragile peace but was often shattered. Raids and counterraids continued for the next 30 years."

"Blas de Hinojos, the commanding general of New Mexico troops, left Santa Fe on a slaving expedition. The most significant fighting force ever sent against the Navajo Nation. Hinojos planned to use the 8000-foot-high Canyon walls to access the Navajo Nation's homes in Canyon de Chelly. However, scouts for the Navajos spotted the dust clouds of the Mexicans crossing the Chaco Wash. The soldier's polished buttons reflected sunlight like Mirrors, costing them the advantage of surprise. Chief Narbona, dressed in his fighting paint, led his warriors into the pass and hid them high in the rocky gap. His warriors waited until the Mexicans entered the canyon. The walls were so steep and narrow that Hinojo's soldiers had to lead their horses on foot. When Chief Narbona gave the signal, the Navajo warriors, who had guns, fired; other warriors rained arrows and showered boulders down on the unprotected troops.

    Chief Narbona said that our warriors killed the Mexicans by cutting a tree trunk into kindling."
    Dolly focused on the next part of her story and said, "The Mexican American War was a conflict between the United States and Mexico, fought from April 1846 to February 1848. The War stemmed from a dispute over the boundaries of the annexation of the Republic of Texas. In 1845, the dispute over Texas ended at the Nueces River. The Mexican claim was for the Rio Grande. The U.S. claim was questioned. Nevertheless, the final disposition favored the United States. "Later, after the United States had wrestled control of the New Mexico

territory, Colonel John Washington led a small army into Navajo Country to bring peace to the area.

"People in Congress were bent on achieving a peace which eluded the Spanish and Mexicans. A Powwow was established. The Navajos were led by Chief Narbona, who brought horses and sheep as gifts. However, during the peace talks, an American trooper accused a Navajo warrior of stealing a horse. Angered by the charge, Chief Narbona prepared to leave. The American troopers fired upon the congregation and killed six warriors, including Chief Narbona.

"Continuous warfare followed until General James Carlton's mission to remove the Navajos from their traditional homeland was initiated and completed. Carlton marched the sorry Navajo natives four hundred miles to the Bosque Redondo. The Long Walk march was in the winter, and many Navajo people died of exposure.

"This disastrous episode ended in 1868 when the treaty was signed by General William T. Sherman and twenty-eight other Navajo headmen, including Chief Narbona's son. The treaty ended the hostilities between the Navajos and the Americans, who turned their attention to subduing the Apaches and other tribes," Dolly concluded her story.

Dolly sat back and drew a long, deep breath; "Charlie, that is the story of two men with the same name. What do you think?

"Well, truth is often much stranger than fiction," stammered Chile Charlie.

# CHAPTER TEN

## *The trip*

At 10:30, Chile Charlie and Dolly were ready to leave Gallup for Window Rock. Charlie said, "We have two options to get to Window Rock. The first would be to continue north to the sacred and surreal Shiprock, then turn west at Four Corners, where Arizona, Colorado, New Mexico, and Utah state lines meet. Or the second option would be to first travel west along I-40W and continue north on I-40W shortly after Lupton. Next, we could take Indian Route 12.

After giving it much thought, they chose the second option, which was the most scenic, and they could discover a small unknown portion of Arizona.

Looking at the map, they realized; that Indian Route 12 crossed into New Mexico, along the state border, and then it re-entered the Grand Canyon State.

They were thrilled to travel on Indian Route 12, and the excitement built as they got closer to Window Rock because they didn't know what to expect from this road that connects to other main roads that give you incredible scenic landscapes.

They were given eye-candy views on our way north through the Navajo Nation. In Arizona, the colors of the reliefs, hills, rock formations, and cavities created by erosion were more vibrant. They had to make frequent stops to take pictures.

Charlie said, "I didn't think we'd find so much to admire and photograph. The changes in the landscape were even more dramatic than I expected."

The small towns give way to endless landscapes accentuated by remarkable rock formations against the blue sky.

As they traveled north along Defiance Plateau, the road led north to Oak Springs and the community of small farms. Then they came across Hunters Point, a wooded area stretching west from the plateau. Hunters Point was named after John Hunter, a superintendent of the southern Navajo jurisdiction.

Charlie said, "Let's make a brief stop at St. Michael's, a mission founded in 1898 by Franciscan priests who used the stone building as their Chapel and residence."

St. Michael's Indian School, founded by the Sisters of the Blessed Sacrament and led by Mother Katherine Drexel, was inaugurated in 1900 with fifty Navajo students.

Mother Drexel gave up a comfortable life as an heir to take her vows. She was canonized as a saint in 2000 by Pope John Paul II.

The stone school building has become a museum, while St. Michael's mission and school still serve the Navajo community. The town, also called St. Michaels, has accommodations, two restaurants, and scenic tours of historical sites. Monoliths, mesas, and high rock spikes have "beaks" on our right.

Then a little further on, they saw more red rocks as they approached Window Rock and the Navajo Nation Museum.

They knew they were about to see something unique approaching Window Rock. About a mile north of the community, they saw the sacred rock formation of the same name. It is a large circular "window" with a diameter of 46 ft., imposing and striking above a 197 ft. high sandstone hill. It's located close to the fenced area with Navajo government buildings, while an open space would have enhanced the view.

They enter the property slowly, meeting no one to ask if they need a permit, and even the offices seem closed. In the green space under the large hole in the rock, an imposing bronze statue almost 16 ft. tall catches our attention. It is a soldier statue that serves as a symbol to honor the legendary Navajo marines whose language was a strategic communication technique in battle during the Second World War.

The memorial also includes bayonets and a circular walkway over the rock. Besides being a spectacular place, Window Rock is home to the Navajo Tribal Museum. Visiting Anasazi ruins nearby on foot or horseback with a guide is possible. Contact the Navajo Nation Parks and Recreation in Window Rock to discover places to go sightseeing.
They continued to drive, not knowing what the landscape would be like on the way to Goosenecks State Park, and this uncertainty makes

us want to keep our cameras out if we see something incredible.

Fortunately, few vehicles pass through this area, which is a point in our favor. They can stop or turn back whenever they want to snap a picture.

Charlie stated, "The beauty of the rocky landscape is breathtaking, but who knows if we will arrive at our destination if we continue like this. Let's do approximate calculations and plan the length of the stops. These places filled with "enchanting silence" contain much history and often have a turbulent past."

Ten miles north of Window Rock, the lush green valley of *Tséhootsooí* (meadow among the rocks) was a peaceful refuge for the Navajo's horses and sheep for years.

Medicinal herbs grew in this sacred land, and water flowed. Then in 1851, the land was confiscated from the Navajo to establish Fort Defiance and used as a base to protect the settlers in the region.
Charlie told Dolly the soldiers called it "Hell's Gate." It was the scene of several battles because of its remote location. It later became a prison camp for

the Navajo before they were driven away from here to go to Bosque Redondo and Fort Sumner in New Mexico. Today, it has become one of the leading centers of the Navajo Nation."

Then, as they headed north on Indian Route 12, they continued past Window Rock. Near Tsaile, they saw "rock fingers" rise towards the sky. As we admire these curious shapes, we realize we always appreciate gazing at this landscape. The landscape is bizarre as if it were another world, but they snapped back into reality when they saw a horse grazing in the distance and sheep around bushes.

Look, Dolly, Charlie said. "In the distance, you can see a Hogan, a characteristic Navajo dwelling. Then in Tsaile, it is possible to visit Diné College, the oldest and largest tribal college, or stop at Tsaile Lake and Tsaile Creek, which continues to flow through Muerto Canyon and Canyon de Chelly."

Speaking of the latter, there was a sign on Indian Route 12 to turn west on Highway 64. They didn't think about it twice; they took a detour on Highway 64 for about eighteen miles.

Charlie quipped, "One advantage of Indian Route 12, besides being unique, is that other scenic roads branch off or continue. They knew they were heading off course, but it seemed fitting to do this because they wanted to have a look.

Who knows how long it'll be until we come back here!"

Dolly said, "I read there was an overlook called Massacre Cave Overlook because, during a Spanish military expedition, 805 Navajo (women and children in particular) were killed when a cave collapsed. They had taken shelter there since in one canyon as their strongholds. You can sometimes see cliffs interspersed with green trees."

They get back on Indian Route 12 and head north. They could see the Lukachukai Mountains and continue their drive, which they declared a treasure trove. What seemed peculiar large rocks from a distance often reveal themselves as beautiful, unique rock formations that transform the scenery. This view is a pure natural beauty! Indian Route 12 is like a long, beautiful tree from which beautiful branches grow. They finally arrived at Round Rock, where a giant monolith and a smaller one marked the end of Indian Route 12 and the beginning of Highway 191.

They imagined or hoped that the route would have a few pleasant surprises in store, and it did. But the journey continued because our destination was Goosenecks State Park. On the way to Goosenecks, the scenery becomes increasingly beautiful. Shortly after crossing the border with Utah, along the horizon line, they see Monument Valley. It seems like a mirage, and as they continue south on Highway 163, it becomes more of a concrete reality.

In Northern Arizona, near Winslow, an hour and a half's drive from Grand Canyon Village, a natural attraction rarely frequented for unknown reasons.

# CHAPTER ELEVEN

*Finally, the arrival*

Chile Charlie and Dolly finally arrived at the Navajo Nation Headquarters at 3:15. They were happy about selecting Indian Route 12 for their trip. The pictures they took were well worth the side trip.

They found the headquarters building and entered the building. The desk clerk gave them directions to the Superintendent's office. Charlie and Dolly were amazed at the size and sturdiest entrance door to the Superintendent's office area.

The door could withstand a frontal strike from the Mongol Army.

The door was made from imported Teak Wood, polished to a high lust. The heavyweight door made it challenging to open with one hand. Charlie used both hands to pry the door open. Dolly and Charlie entered the ultra-spacious office of Mr. Wayne Dawson, the Regional Superintendent of the Navajo Nation.

Dolly and Chile Charlie, at the direction of Mr. Dawson, took seats in front of his desk. The chairs were brown leather overstuffed recliners and were amazingly comfortable. There was an extended writing platform attached if needed.

Mr. Dawson politely asked, "Of what service can I be to you, wonderful people?"

Dawson was Navajo from stem to stern. Large, firm looking, erect, dressed in Western clothing. His physical features fit his melodious baritone voice.

Chile Charlie leaned forward and stated, "There have been two unsolved murders of Navajo men in Gallup. We think there may be a connection between the murders and the Navajo personal revenge tradition. It may be a long shot, but we wondered if we might get some help researching any clan or tribe connections that may lead to solving these murders."

"That's interesting," Dawson murmured as he stroked his chin.

"I will give you some background concerning our records and where others may be found," Wayne told Charlie and Dolly. She leaned forward to listen, but Charlie sat motionlessly.

Mr. Wayne Dawson explained, "The Navajo Nation is the largest federally recognized tribe in the United States. The Navajo Nation is an independent government body that manages the Navajo reservations. Like most groups, the Navajos relate their history to remarkable events that influenced their people, and family history information usually relates to these events.

In 1936, Window Rock, Arizona, was chosen as the site for the Navajo Central Agency. The Navajo Tribal Council is the lead agency so that we can access data in our computer files. If our information would help solve a murder mystery of the dead Navajos, I will permit you to use the database."

"One roadblock with determining Navajo's heritage is the scarcity of a written language. Chile Charlie added that such languages were passed on orally, which allowed for changes," Chile Charlie added.

"Like any other civilization, precautionary steps were taken to limit intermarriages among immediate family members. The Navajo established family clans with the predominant maternal line. When introducing oneself, a Navajo will provide their parent's clan and typically their maternal grandfather and paternal grandfather's clan. This introduction established their place in the world. Knowing one's clans is just as important as knowing the names of past ancestors and goes together with genealogical research.

When dealing with Navajo clan records, you can contact government offices that have dealt with Navajo tribes. The three primary levels of offices included are Indian agents, Superintendent, and Commissioner of Indian Affairs," Mr. Dawson said.

He stood and looked down at his guests, "The United States and Native American relations began with the first acts of the Continental Congress in 1775, which passed several ordinances dealing with indigenous people. The first was to divide administrative responsibility into three geographical districts. There were the northern, central, and southern regions.

A Superintendent was created to govern the affairs between Congress and the Navajo people. Often ex-officio Superintendent of Indian Affairs was usually held by Territorial governors who would help negotiate and get titles to land. Multiple tribes lived in territorial boundaries; agents governed one or more tribes or geographical areas. The President, with approving the Senate, appointed Indian agents. Agents were to report to the

Superintendent, but the records were sent directly to Washington D.C," Dawson explained.

"The Bureau of Indian Affairs (BIA) was created in 1824 as part of the War Department to govern the affairs between settlers and many Native people, including the Navajo. Called Heads of the Bureau of Indian Affairs initially, this title was later changed to Commissioner of Indian Affairs and has since been changed to Assistant Secretary of the Interior of Indian Affairs. When natives were no longer considered a threat, the BIA was transferred to the Department of the Interior in 1849 and continues today," Dawson clarified.

"Are most records of individuals available to us, or do we have to go through the tribal headquarters," asked Dolly.

"Is there a local office of the Bureau of Indian Affairs and were charged with maintaining records of those activities under their responsibility," Chile Charlie probed.

Dawson said, "Now, among these records are the Navajo Nation's reservations boundaries that have been changed since the original reservation boundaries were established in 1868. **The Navajo Nation is divided into five agencies governing a specific geographical area, with the seat of** government here. Each agency is further divided into smaller political units called Chapters; the number of Chapters has fluctuated over the years, but there are roughly 110 Chapters. Typically, Chapters do not carry documents containing family history information, and most will refer you to the Navajo Nation offices. Besides this, records held at the agencies have also been transferred to National and Regional archives throughout the United States.

Like most civilizations, geography played a crucial role in Navajo life, as did mythology, religion, and history. Today, reservations in the United States of America establish boundaries. Over time, those boundaries have changed.

Learning local history can also help with understanding family history. Boundaries for the Navajo Nation Reservation are about 24,078,127 square miles, making it the largest reservation in the United States. It covers parts of Arizona, New Mexico, and Utah. There are also three entities under Navajo authority.

Tribal lands are trusted lands with no private landowners, and all Tribal Trust land is owned in common and administered by the Nation's government. There are also BIA Indian Allotment lands privately owned by the heirs and generations of the original BIA Indian Allotted to whom it was issued.

Tribal Trust lands are leased to customary land users and may include home sites, grazing, and other uses."

Wayne Dawson pointed at the map on the wall; here is a Navajo Nation Public Service Map.

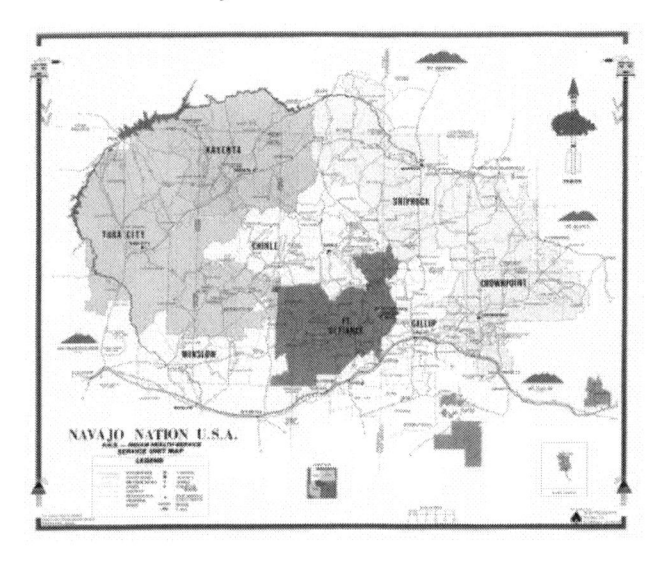

Dawson continued, "The Superintendent of Indian affairs oversaw Indian agents. As for the Navajo Nation, superintendents conflicted with who held authority over areas occupied by the Navajos. Neighboring superintendents also assisted governing superintendents over the Navajos. Over time territorial boundaries also shifted and changed. The New Mexico and Arizona Superintendence are the principal record-holders for Navajos.

Two types of census records are available for people searching for Native American records. The first is the U.S. decennial census records and Indian Census Rolls, which have identical information and some differences. Indian Census records were usually taken by agents or superintendents in charge of Indian reservations and then sent to the Commissioner of Indian Affairs, as required by the Act of July 4, 1884.

By 1940, many areas covered under the Indian Census Rolls were soon incorporated into U.S. decennial census records.

Because of several issues surrounding the land, the federal government, especially with the Indian Reorganization Act of 1934 (a.k.a Wheeler-Howard Act), encouraged Navajos to determine their membership and enrollment. The question before the Navajos was, "Who is a Navajo?" To help move the issue along, Blood Quantum was introduced as a requirement for tribal membership, allowing tribes to select ancestry for an individual to be considered part of a specific tribe. As for the Navajos, those that had one-fourth blood for membership were selected.

President Franklin D. Roosevelt signed the legislation as part of his New Deal policy. But, for the Navajo Nation, it was their New Deal. It improved the social and economic conditions of the Navajos.

Those enrolled in a federally recognized tribe are given a Certificate Degree of Indian Blood and are assigned an Indian Census Number unique to each individual. Knowing your relatives' Indian Census numbers can be helpful when searching the Indian Census Rolls and can help eliminate confusion, but not all Indian Census Roll takers include censuses. The U.S. decennial census taker would have Census Numbers in their records.

The National Archives Microfilm Publication M595 has copies of the Indian Census Rolls, containing about 692 rolls dealing with many tribes in the United States. Indian Census Roll takers were instructed to include an individual's Indian and English names.

By 1902 instruction was given that families should be given the same surname and that they should translate Indian names into English if they were too difficult to pronounce or remember. If names were too "foolish, cumbersome or uncouth translations that would handicap a self-respecting person should not be tolerated," derogatory nicknames were dropped and changed.

When searching Indian Census Rolls, you must be mindful that they are divided into one of four central agencies; Eastern, Southern, Western, Northern, and smaller ones.

Others can be found in other tribal census records; Apache, Hopi, Ute, Paiute, and others.

The Online Indian Census Rolls can be found at Ancestry.com. This website has all the benefits of searching records from the comforts of home. They have only a few Indian Census Rolls available for Navajo records. Family History Libraries can be more time-consuming but provide more information left out by online sites. Online sites only include the names of individuals and leave out a wealth of information at the beginning of the census rolls, including special instructions and procedures by the census taker and even census maps.

The United States Federal Population Census records regarding Navajo Indigenous People are varied by area. From about 1885 until 1930, Natives had to be placed on Indian Census Rolls. By 1940 they were incorporated into U.S. federal population census records.

Navajos were placed on U.S. federal population census records in some areas as early as 1900 and are usually limited to Natives living in or around border towns. As most know, U.S. federal population census records are recorded every ten years and include Indian Census Numbers and can help track down ancestors.

One major issue when dealing with these records is that there were Census takers who were not Navajo speakers and relied on translators for information.

In addition, when these censuses were taken, Navajo was still becoming an official written language, so many Census takers phonetically printed names. Census takers often printed generic names for people using Navajo terms such as; "At'eed" (girl); "Ashkii, (boy); and "Asdzaan" (woman) or Hastiin (mister or man).

When searching U.S. Federal Indian Census records, their records are divided into reservation boundaries which include: Navajo, Pueblo Bonito, located around Chaco Canyon, NM, and San Juan, situated around northern San Juan County, NM, which attended Bureau of Indian Affairs schools (boarding schools), public schools, and contract schools (mission schools). Each has records that have found their way into archives and historical societies. The Office of Indian Affairs (now Bureau of Indian Affairs) provided educational opportunities for Navajo pupils and identified them through school census records and other means.

Newspapers provide a wealth of information besides local happenings; birth, death, and even marriage notifications can be found in local newspapers around the Navajo reservation. Each paper is held at various libraries, depositories, and institutions in different states. Here is a list of newspapers around the reservation that deal specifically with the Navajo but are not limited to this list:

The Navajo have a polytheistic belief system that dictates how to treat oneself, others, and one's environment. This belief system has helped them deal with groups of people entering the Navajo country. As the Spanish penetrated present-day New Mexico and Arizona, they introduced Spanish Christianity to the Navajos. Documentation from Spanish sources includes Navajo names, but the names usually need to be more generic to pinpoint ancestors. Mexican documentation also has this shortcoming.

By the late 1800s, The Church of Jesus Christ of Latter-day Saints (a.k.a Mormons) moved into and settled in southern Utah, Arizona, and western New Mexico. The Navajos called these people *Gaamalii* (the fat ones coming). Mission records, missionaries, and settlers wrote journals and diaries that can include Navajo family names. Baptismal and Church membership records are harder to come by and usually limited to Church members.

But baptismal and church membership records in earlier times are minimal. When Navajos were incorporated into the church, the church did not have plans to establish or maintain religious contact with the Navajos unless there was a dire need.

As the United States gained control over present-day New Mexico and Arizona, they assigned religious groups to the different tribes. The Presbyterians or Protestants ministers were appointed to the Navajo reservation.

Language Family Correlations were a second factor. It was based on language families. Due to wars and migrations of people, languages often intermingle with other families. A language family consists of similar languages and has a common origin.

Regarding Native North Americans, a handful of language families seem to dominate. There are clues. Language families consist of similar languages and have a common origin. Language has a way of changing."

Dolly informed Charlie, "Even in written language, consider that the English of 1,000 years ago is hardly recognizable to modern English speakers today. Consider also that Australian English did not even exist two hundred years ago! So, although the language family may help identify relationships of various tribes and nations, it still may not be enough to tie these language families directly back to their ancestors."

Charlie stood, stretched, put his hands over his head, and backed down, "Mr. Dawson, you told us we could access your data files. If that offer still stands, when and where can we start?

Mr. Dawson said as he left, "We have the data you might find on our computers housed in this building. If you give me an hour, I can have the room available. In the meantime, make yourselves comfortable in the Break Lounge across the hall. There is coffee, tea, soda, and water there; help yourself. I will meet you there in an hour with the keys.

"Keys?"

"Yes, we close the building at five, but you are welcome to stay as long as you like, doing your research. There is a key for the data room and one for the outside door. You can return the keys in the morning."

Dawson was gone.

Charlie turned to Dolly, "Let's not waste our time sitting around twiddling our thumbs. Let's use your analytical skills to plan what to do once we enter the data room. We can do that while we're waiting in the lounge."

"Why are you sitting there, Charlie? Let's go," Dolly teased. And off they went to the lounge.

They sat side by side, Dolly softly touching Charlie's shoulder, desiring the human touch but not showing too much affection. Charlie was not into *lovie movie* stuff now. He was on a mission.

"Dolly, you are more experienced at analytic research than I am. We know the names of the murder victims and their clans right now. That's it. Where should we start?"

Dolly smiled and spoke, "Questions are where we start. What do you want or need to discover? Maybe, we should try to find out who owned what track of land and when they owned it. I'm sure you know that land ownership means much to the Navajos. They have been pushed around for years by the whites and the Hopi and Apache Indians. That could be a motivation for revenge killing."

Dawson returned with the promised keys. "Here you are, happy hunting; see you two in the morning, and he was gone.

Chile Charlie and Dolly grabbed their quickly scribbled notes and went directly to the data room. A desktop and two laptop computers were stationed near the far wall with reading lamps to provide adequate lighting. Much to his surprise, Charlie could open the desktop computer without a password. Dolly did the same at the laptop on the right side of Charlie.

Both stared at their computer screens hoping that by untold magic, looking would give them an inkling of what they were supposed to discover. Dolly fidgeted; she did not know what she was supposed to find, making her uneasy.

After Chile, Charlie stood up to stretch, making no discoveries that would lead to any connection between the Native American corpses. He turned to Dolly and said, "Let's call it a day and go back to Gallup, have supper, rest, and come back tomorrow. What do you say is that a good plan or not?"

Dolly muttered, "That is just fine with me, Charlie. I just can't get into this idea of finding something to link these two murderers."

They quickly gathered up their meager belongings and left and locked the data room door. They found their way to the exit and left. Charlie took the keys out of his pocket and secured the lock on the outer door.

Charlie and Dolly drove in complete silence back to Gallup. Both were wondering how they might use the data available. They had yet to decide what they could find right now. They didn't have a plan. Once they arrived, Charlie asked, "Are you hungry, Dolly? If you are, let's get a quick bite to eat, retire for the night, and start early tomorrow morning.

"Yes, Charlie, I am starved. We haven't had anything to eat since the early afternoon. Don't forget we go split bill." And they proceeded to the dining room, sat down, and waited for the waiter to bring their usual two glasses of water. Both ordered tea as a nightcap. They asked the waiter if they could order from the breakfast menu. The waiter said, "Yes, they could." They ordered bacon, eggs, and toast from the breakfast menu. "Dolly, maybe after a good night's rest, we can devise a plan to learn if there is any connection between those murders," Charlie said as they finished their tea and food.

"See you at breakfast at eight in the morning, and then we will be off," Dolly said as they left for their rooms.

The following day, Chile Charlie arrived at the hotel restaurant first. Dolly came almost immediately and took a seat across from Charlie. She looked refreshed, with a smile of contentment on her face, ready for a full day of data research. They ordered a heavy pancake breakfast, knowing they might have a full day of research. After breakfast, they left for their rooms to pick up their clothes and materials for the day.

Today's drive to the Navajo Nation Headquarters differed from last night's silent trip. Both could not stop stepping on each other's talking points as they journeyed. They laughed. Chile Charlie said, "Ladies first." Their discussions centered on the sun's golden coloring of the rocky landscape. Dolly employed her vast academic vocabulary in her descriptions. Charlie nodded his head in agreement as the journey continued.

▲▲▲▲▲

"Coffee first, then to the data room," Charlie informed Dolly. She acknowledged agreement to the plan with a quick gesture of her head.

Charlie unlocked the door; both went directly to their computers. Charlie opened the Navajo Times site, and Dolly opened the ancestry. They stared at the screen and jotted down keywords to start the inquiry.

"Dolly, here is what we know," Chile Charlie said.

"The first victim's name was Red Deer, a Navajo from the Crown Point clan. The second body belonged to Edwardo Yellow Skin, a Navajo from one of the Tohatchi area tribes. Both were killed with a sharp object, much like a Bowie knife." If I'm not mistaken, each body was discovered in the exact location. Is that your recollection? "Yes," Dolly whispered.

Dolly, I will start a search of land transfers from 1950 until today to see if the names appear on the records. You could look at the ancestry linkages to determine any relationship between the two murders.

The efforts of both Charlie and Dolly would undoubtedly classify as looking for a needle in a haystack. This search would be a long and laborious task without guaranteed favorable results. The only thing that could be assured would be tired eyeballs.

Dolly said, "Charlie, I have to take a break. I will enter the lounge, sit with a hot cup of coffee, and rest my eyes. Do you want to join me, or do you want me to bring you coffee?"

Charlie got up, stretched his arms over his head, and took a deep breath, "I will join you in the lounge for a cup of coffee. I did not find newspaper information that would provide a clue about land transfers or other hints to show any direct linkage between the two Native Americans. But I did find land transfers that involved both the Hopis and the Navajos. Unfortunately, there were none under the names of the murdered Indians."

"I had the same misfortune," Dolly said. "What should we do now? Shall we quiet?" Charlie glanced at Dolly; "I am not sure but know I will finish my coffee and walk around the block before I give you my opinion. There has to be an answer somewhere in the data."

Charlie returned from his walk to find Dolly sitting in the lounge. She looked unhappy. Charlie sat next to Dolly.

He said, "I know you are discouraged about this search. But as I was walking, I was reminded of our conversation several days ago about the Indian Reorganization Act of 1934. I will examine the possibilities that might lead us to a new search direction.

"Are you with me?"

"I guess so," Dolly answered, and they proceeded back into the data room.

▲▲▲▲▲

In 1974, a memorandum from Ken Cole to the President of the United States for the Navajo Hopi land settlement issue. It was dated December 24, 1974, and provided a framework for settling the significant land dispute between the Navajos and the Hopi Indians. Of most concern was an area where the Hopi village of Moenkopi was located on the Navajo reservation.

"The conflict originated in differing cultural patterns of the two tribes. The Hopis were sedentary village people, in other words, farmers. Whereas the Navajos were semi-nomadic, roaming the area as freely as possible. This cultural difference caused hostilities," Chile Charlie said he had read, and you, Dolly, confirmed the hypothesis earlier.

Dolly said, "OK, but that doesn't get us further in solving the two murderers. It only gives us more information about the hostilities. How will we be able to solve this matter by researching this data? It doesn't make sense to me."

"You're right, Dolly. Let's check with the police department to see if they have found any new clues. Pack up your notes, and let's head back to Gallup.

# CHAPTER TWELVE

*One solution, new problem*

Chile Charlie and Dolly Sweet Thompson arrived at the Gallup Police Department early the following day. They asked the sergeant in charge to talk to the Chief of police.

They talked of the Navajo mythology and how much Charlie knew about it on their return to Gallup. Dolly talked a little and slept quite a bit, and when she awoke, she was full of questions. She wanted to know just how much knowledge of Navajo myths he learned and where he learned it. There was the question of how human intelligence works and the difference between the mind and the brain. "That's just too much to digest right now; let's call it a day," Charlie expounded.

Chile Charlie and Dolly Sweet Thompson arrived at the Gallup Police Department early the following day. Dolly put her purse on the rolling inspection device and stepped through the metal detector. Charlie emptied his pockets, removed his belt, and passed through the metal detector. They saw the sergeant in charge behind the plexiglass cubical with a microphone. Charlie said, "We want to talk to Chief Henry Trefren."

"Take a seat, and I'll check with the Chief to see if he's available. He has had a busy schedule today." Fine, Charlie answered and stepped away to sit with Dolly.

"Step this way; Chief Trefern will see you," the desk Sargent commanded.

With a wave, the Chief welcomed Dolly and Chile Charlie into his spacious office. "Please have a seat," Chief Trefern said. They took four steps and sat in the fifteen-minute chairs in front of the Chief's large walnut desk with *Gallup Police Department* engraved in the front center. On the wall behind his desk were three glass-enclosed shadow boxes. One box was filled with arm patches from other New Mexico community police departments. The second shadowbox contained police identification badges, and the third included pictures of wanted criminals.

The area behind Dolly and Charlie had a circular table with six chairs surrounding it.

"What can I do for you today," the Chief queried.

"Dolly and I are here to discuss the murders of the two Indians found here last week." We have been trying to determine why the murders took place and who did them. We know that the Gallup Police Department is also investigating these murders, and we wanted to know if you made any progress," Charlie said.

Chief Trefren turned from somber to a broad smile and said, "Yes, we have solved those two murders but opened a box of worms because a third murder has occurred. One of our officers, Detective Red Rope, killed the two Native Americans found last week. He killed the Navajo and Hopi victims as a revenge killing. Red Rope thought their clans took land away from their tribe during the land transfers as part of the Reorganization Act of 1934 and amended in 1974. But he was then murdered, and we have absolutely no idea why."

"The life of law enforcement officers continues baffling," Chile Charlie whispered to himself. "Thanks, Chief. Dolly and I will leave you so you can solve the murder of Detective Red Rope."

"I am returning to Las Cruces after I take you to lunch. It has been a pleasure these past weeks,"

Chile Charlie said as he put his arms around Dolly Sweet Thompson.

## THE END

# ADVENTURE THREE

## *NAVAJO TRADITIONAL SPIRITUAL BELIEFS*

### Chapter One

### Tohatchi Day One

Dolly Thompson sprang to her feet as Liv Hernandez concluded his presentation. She joined the packed house audience in their standing ovation for his comparative Native American Spiritual Beliefs speech. Hernandez was the Dean of the Archaeology Department at Chicago Loyola University. Dolly was a third-year candidate for Doctor's degree there. The Ph.D. degree will be in the bag when she completes writing her dissertation.

▲▲▲▲▲

Three days later, Dolly was in the office of her dissertation lead professor, Dr. Jimmy Samson. "Dolly, I read the first four chapters of your Navajo Spiritual Beliefs dissertation project. I found the information intriguing, but the information is secondhand. I suggest you obtain some first-hand data," Dr. Samson recommended.

"Yes, I understand the work could be enhanced with actual face-to-face interviews, but I am on a limited budget. Are there any funds available to help me?" Dolly inquired.

"I'm not sure; let me look into a research grant for you," he said. "Come back in two weeks; I will surely have your answer."

Dolly left the office in high spirits thinking she had a chance to spend time in the northwest corner of New Mexico again.

The two weeks passed like a snail crossing a road. She entered Samson's office and took a seat across from Dr. Samson. His white teeth showed through his big smile.

"Dolly, good news. The department is interested in your research. They have appropriated $15,000 for you to continue your first-hand interviews with the Navajos. There is one caveat they placed upon the grant. They would like for you to explore in depth the Skinwalkers myth within the Navajo tribes. If you would please sign this document, I will voucher the money so you can research the information about the Skinwalkers," Dr. Samson responded.

"Yes, I would add the Skinwalkers' information to my research project and continue my study of the similarities and differences between the Western

Bible and the Navajo Spiritual Beliefs. Thank you very much for your help. I look forward to completing my dissertation as soon as possible," Dolly said. She felt giddy as she left the office.

▲▲▲▲▲▲

On Dolly's first visit to Gallup, she and Chile Charlie became friends when a stranger broke into Dolly's room and demanded money. She sought help from a hotel guest, Chile Charlie. That incident was the beginning of their friendship.

Dolly found Chile Charlie's phone number in her address book. *I will ask him to meet me at the El Rancho Hotel.* She made the call. "Charlie, surprise, this is Dolly. I am going to be in Gallup in two weeks. I would like you to join me there," she stated.

"Why?" Charlie probed.

"I received a research grant to gather more data for my dissertation. I must add first-hand information about the similarities and differences between the Western Bible and Navajo Spiritual Beliefs. The professors also want me to gather information about the Skinwalkers myth. From my previous experience, I am leery of being alone. Would you be my protector, please," Dolly pleaded.

"My schedule is clear. It would be another adventure. I will meet you in two weeks," Charlie answered.

▲▲▲▲▲

Today could be a dream come true for Dolly Sweet Thompson. She thought the Creation story in the Bible was both similar and different from the Navajo Spiritual Beliefs. During this trip, she hoped to obtain first-hand information clarifying her thesis, and she would finish her dissertation, including details about Skinwalkers.

Dolly asked Chile Charlie to take her to The Chapter House in Tohatchi. He stated he would be delighted to take her. They shook hands and agreed that they looked forward to this new adventure.

At 10 am, they were on their way to Tohatchi. Each wore a comfortable outfit. Chile Charlie was dressed in a red and white checkered shirt, tan cargo pants, and a new black leather vest. Dolly donned a white long-sleeve blouse, fitted black pants, a blue cardigan sweater, and black pumps.

The morning sunlight streamed through the slant-molded cloud cover, casting long eternal beams towards the ground, bathing Chile Charlie and Dolly in a holy crimson light as they walked to his El Camino.

Charlie estimated the drive to Tohatchi would take twenty minutes. Dolly had arranged to meet Painted Cloud, a Navajo Shaman with the Long Step Tribe, at the Tohatchi Chapter House at two o'clock this afternoon.

The Chapter House is located on the eastern flatland portion of the Chuska Mountains and served as the Diné's lifeblood. The Navajos held land usage and other important meetings there.

The recently paved road made for a comfortable ride to the Chapter House. Charlie pulled over to the side of the road. From there, Charlie saw the sunbaked rocks and peaks of the Chuska Mountains while pinon trees spotted the gray hillside. "Isn't that a picture of beauty?"

"I guess so if you are into rocks," Dolly answered.

"In the past, Tohatchi served as a rendezvous place and still holds that distinction today," Dolly added.

"What makes the area important to the Navajo people?" Charlie asked.

"Good question, Charlie," Dolly said. "The Navajos believe the mountains provided the food and medicines for the Creation of the First Woman and Man. The area provided a livelihood for the Navajos and other Native American tribes. The mountain offered everything from skins to food and protection from their enemies."

▲▲▲▲▲

Their drive was comfortable and relaxed. They arrived at 11:30, but the meeting wasn't until two in the afternoon -- a planning error on Charlie's part.

"Have any suggestions for killing three hours before our meeting, Charlie?" asked Dolly. "Let's look for a café for lunch and coffee."

They drove for fifteen minutes, looking for a place to get coffee and eat lunch. But there was not a restaurant or café in Tohatchi.

"Okay, let's go to the Cocina de Domingo Restaurant in Window Rock, Arizona. The food and atmosphere are good, and it is only a twenty-mile drive," Dolly agreed, "but only if we split the bill."

"You're on," Charlie said.

They drove below the speed limit to view and enjoy the incredible rock formations. One formation they named 'Hole in the Wall' and others 'Navajo Warriors.'

Dolly asked Charlie to stop. "Please take some pictures for me," Dolly stated. Charlie stopped and took out his new Sony camera. He shot several pictures of the rock formations.

*Pictures were from the Internet.*

The wind and rain erosion created eye candy on each side of the road. "I am glad we decided to make this drive," Dolly whispered as she glanced at each new rock formation. "I am beginning to like rocks."

The bright sunlight dimmed slightly as the shadows of the midday thunderhead over the Chuska mountains moved across the landscape.

The shadows were the cloud's advanced guard of a soft, cool breeze. The inside of the El Camino cooled briefly. Dolly said, "That was a welcome relief for a moment."

"Yes, clouds can be valuable in the desert.

It took longer than the usual twenty-five minutes to drive to Window Rock. They arrived at 12:15. After being seated. Charlie ordered fried bread with melted cheese as an appetizer to share. Dolly ordered an authentic Navajo meal – tomato-sauté broiled on blue corn mush. Charlie ordered the same, except with goat meat.

*As they waited for their meals, Charlie wondered what was in store for him for the rest of the day. Dolly is a fine traveling companion. But did she want to grasp more about the changing Navajo beliefs or something else?*

The lunchtime sun sneaked through a small gap in the blinds trying to poke its way into the restaurant. The bright red, yellow, and turquoise-colored walls added to the pleasant atmosphere.

"This place reminds me of a café in Juarez that I visited years ago," Dolly told Charlie.

He was not paying attention to her ramblings. Charlie was interested in the sharply dressed young ladies parading past their table.

"A penny for your thoughts. You were in dreamland," Dolly teased.

Before Charlie could answer, their meals arrived on large homemade pottery plates. On the outer edge of each dish were typical Navajo symbols. They ate in silence for a moment.

Dolly admired the symbols on their plates. She pointed to them and said, "These symbols are rooted in tradition, family, and pride. The Navajo are people who lead dedicated lifestyles. These Native American tribes are tethered to their beliefs and regard Navajo symbols as paramount. These Navajo symbols are visible in their pottery and other Navajo art."

"For example, the Kokopelli presides over childbirth and agriculture. Often depicted as a flute player, Kokopelli has an affinity for tricks. This god is also affiliated with music. The sun in the Navajo culture, sunshine is synonymous with good cheer. The sun symbol embodies universal harmony. At its core, this symbol exemplifies high spirits and good fortune. And the Thunderbird is displayed as an outpouring of happiness. In other words, when blessings are bountiful, the Thunderbird appears. The Thunderbird can also stand for serenity," Dolly explained.

Charlie nodded like he agreed but was more interested in his food.

"Is the food as good as you thought it would be," Charlie asked. "Mine is delicious."

With her mouth full, Dolly mumbled, "You bet it's wonderful; you did good, Charlie."

They finished their lunch and started back to Tohatchi. Charlie had a promising idea. "Why don't we take our time getting back to the village? We can see the rock formations we missed on the way here.

"Dolly, do you know of any outstanding stories about Navajos from the village?"

"Yes, Manuelito, the famous Navajo chief, was from Tohatchi. He tried to make peace with the whites. But during the negotiations, settlers accuse Navajos of stealing their cattle. That ended those talks," Dolly said.

"A year later, he negotiated the Treaty of 1869, which brought peace between his people and the whites. That Treaty established the Navajo reservation. The area for his people was smaller than they had claimed before 1864. The Navajos were not accustomed to confinement in a limited area to farm or roam. As always, the Navajos were herding people."

Dolly took a drink and continued, "During these years, chief Manuelito was an influential leader of the Navajo tribes. He encouraged his people to learn the ways of the white man -- it was a better choice than to fight them and lose."

"He taught the Navajos not to resist injustice without educating themselves. He wanted to do as a white man did to overcome his people's oppression. Manuelito was disheartened when the United States government forced the Navajos off their land.

"Government forces led them to the Bosque Redondo near Fort Sumner, New Mexico, which became their new living area. Many members of the tribe died during the move, and others passed away in the harsh Bosque Redondo."

Dolly said, "The land at Bosque Redondo was not suited for farming, and the Navajo prisoners faced deprivation, starvation, disease, and death. By November 1864, about 8,570 people were imprisoned at 'Wheedle,' the Navajo (Diné) word for Bosque Redondo."

"Do you know how long the Navajos were retained there," Charlie asked.

"It was three years, between 1863 and 1866. More than 10,000 Navajo (Diné) were forcibly moved to the Bosque Redondo Reservation."

"During the 'Long Walk,' the U.S. military marched Navajo (Diné) men, women, and children between 250 to 1450 miles, depending on their route. As Navajos faced deteriorating conditions, news of the internment camp spread," Dolly answered.

"Later, the United States government returned the Navajos to the area now known as the Navajo Nation."

♦♦♦♦♦

Again, Charlie and Dolly arrived at the Chapter House earlier than planned. They still had forty minutes before the meeting. Dolly did not want to sit in the hot sun. "Come on, Charlie, let's get inside where it's cooler," Dolly suggested.

An eight-foot chain-link fence surrounded the building. There was no gate to control pedestrian traffic in and out of the facility. *That defeats the whole purpose of the fence, Charlie thought.*

The lobby was more comfortable and relaxed. Racks lined the wall. They were filled with travel brochures for tourists. While waiting, Charlie read several travel brochures which provided historical background information.

Dolly felt a surge of warm air as the front door swung open. Two men entered the lobby. One dressed in a white shirt with a red tie, a light blue suit jacket, pressed tan no-pleat pants, and black crocodile boots. He had long dark hair and dark eyes. His full beard was cut in a goatee style.

"You must be Dolly from Chicago. I am Painted Cloud," he said in his baritone voice. "I am a Shaman for the Navajo Nation. Glad to finally meet you in person."

Chile Charlie noticed that Painted Cloud seemed nervous. His eyes wandered as if he was concerned about being followed.

"This is Blue Rope," Painted Cloud said as he pointed to the gentleman behind him. "He's also a Navajo Shaman."

Blue Rope wore an authentic Kachina outfit. A mask covered his face. His eyes were hidden behind the darkness of the mask. Under his right feather-winged arm, he carried a small gourd bucket.

"Welcome to Tohatchi," Blue Rope said in a chicken-like squawking voice.

"Thank you for inviting us to your headquarters," Dolly responded. "We want to learn the similarities and differences between the Western Bible and the Navajo Spiritual Beliefs."

The front door opened again, and two men entered.

Painted Cloud introduced Dolly and Charlie to Pastor Dan Smith and Padre Damon O'Roke.

"I invited them to join us. They can add valuable information and insights into your comparative study," Painted Cloud said.

Pastor Smith was tall and lean. His face was expressionless, stoic, and rigid, like it was carved in granite. He looked more like a cowboy than a pastor.

He wore a ten-gallon hat, a red and white-striped shirt, faded blue jeans, and cowboy boots.

"Happy to meet both of you," he said. His voice was loud and croaky, like a bullfrog calling for its mate.

Padre O'Roke was a twenty-nine-year-old priest who had a receding hairline. He wore a black short-sleeve shirt with a white cleric collar, and his pants and wing-tipped shoes were also black.

"He was from Juarez, Mexico, and assigned to the St. Patrick's Church a year ago. The Padre seldom says much because of his limited command of English," Painted Cloud said as he started to walk away.

Dolly and Charlie followed Painted Cloud. Everyone else followed behind. The sign on the side of the entrance door read ROADRUNNER CONFERENCE ROOM. It was a large room with a rectangular conference table set for sixteen people.

The room was lit with fluorescent lighting, and the air-conditioning was doing an excellent job. It kept the room at a comfortable seventy-two degrees. Everyone comfortably sat on the leather-swivel chairs.

Painted Cloud pretended he was a waiter and took everyone's drink order. While waiting for the drinks, Charlie examined the sand and other oil paintings on the wall.

"Are all these original works of local artists?" Charlie asked.

"Yes, they are," Blue Rope slowly answered. "We are a proud people. Art plays a major part in our culture. The Navajo artists provide artistic work that preserves it."

Painted Cloud returned with the drinks. Padre O'Roke held his glass out in a salute to everyone present. The others did likewise. "Cheers to everyone," Painted Cloud announced.

Chile Charlie was eager to start -- He grew up in the Midwest, where people get to the point without significant trivia talk.

Standing, Dolly initiated the meeting. She stated, "In the research for my dissertation, I studied historical documents. I wrote about the Spiritual Beliefs of various Native American tribes. My work was from secondary sources. Now, I want to add firsthand information to the work I gather while here.

"I know that your ancestors came here when Navajos, along with the other Native American groups, originally came to North and South America because of the dispersion at the Tower of Babel," Dolly stated.

"Yes, Genesis 10 records the migration routes of developing nations and territories. There was a description of the division of people and their moving to other places, including the Americas," Pastor Dan Smith explained.

He continued, "There was some mixing and extension of family groups, but they had little choice—they had to move. All groups took the knowledge of a God, the Flood, proper worship, and the false worship practiced at Babel. In those groups were individuals with special skills to form new cultures."

"There are documents describing the resulting efforts recognizable today," Padre O'Roke offered.

"Other family groups adopted a hunter-gatherer mode of existence."

"Like the Navajos who settled in the great Southwest. They were not ignorant savages. They were smart because their God created them that way," Painted Cloud said.

▲▲▲▲▲

"Let us move on to more developments if we can," Chile Charlie pushed.

Dolly continued, "Please tell us about any conflicts between Spain's appointed governors and the Navajo tribes."

Pastor Smith addressed her question, saying, "Don Juan de Onate was the son of wealthy silver mining parents from Zacatecas, New Spain. He gained more prominence when he married the granddaughter of Herman Cortez."

"June 1598, he led a contingency of settlers north from Mexico City and traveled through the *Jornada del Muerte*, an inhospitable patch of desert. He wanted to spread Roman Catholicism by establishing new missions in Nuevo Mexico."

"To serve as the colony's governor, he had to pay the King of Spain for the privilege. Onate wanted to find a way to recoup his investment. At the same time, he wanted to make enough profit to live leisurely for the rest of his life. But early settlers found no gold to pay the King in the colony."

"Using the military to enslave the Navajo tribes, Onate compelled them to work. Like many other governors, he was ruthless in treating the Indian people."

Padre O'Roke searched for the right words and then spoke. "The priests struggled to curtail the greed and oppression of Onate. They sought to convert the Navajo population to Christianity. This would require a church - not just any- but an edifice reminiscent of the churches in Spain. They needed funds to build and maintain the church."

"The priests had the Navajo servants, farmers, and herders as a ready and reasonable labor force. Their abuse of the Navajo tribes was no less offensive than Onate's."

"What happened to Don Juan Onate," Charlie wanted to know.

"The King of Spain removed Onate from authority. He was charged with mismanagement and abuse of the Navajos," Painted Cloud responded.

Charlie looked up at the small windows high above the west wall. He noticed the sun's orange glow fade as it slid below the horizon. He turned to Dolly and the others, saying, "We're going to return to Gallup now, and we will return at nine in the morning to continue our talks."

▲▲▲▲▲

Darkness was fast approaching as Charlie and Dolly were returning to Gallup.

Charlie broke the silence. "What did you think about today's session?"

Dolly answered, "It was a good icebreaker session. The group provided valuable information to build an in-depth foundation for the subject."

"Spoken like a real academic, I felt naked without my Bible. I forgot it when I was packing to come to Gallup. I will purchase one tonight if we can find a bookstore open," Charlie said.

"Don't worry; there is always a Walmart with a book section," Dolly said.

"Let's have dinner at the hotel. Then I will go to Walmart to buy a Bible," Charlie added.

▲▲▲▲▲

It was after eight when Charlie entered the vast Walmart building. He asked the greeter the location of the book section. The greeter motioned to the next aisle and said, "To the very back of the store."

Charlie did a military right face and briskly walked to the appointed aisle. He started his long march to the book section. When he arrived, he saw a tall man looking over the fiction section. Charlie asked, "Sir, can you help me find the religious section? I'm looking for a Bible to purchase."

The man said, "Of course, I am familiar with the books here. I can help you. Take three steps, turn to your left, and you will be in the section designated as religious literature."

"Thank you," Charlie said as he turned, took the three steps, and found the religious section of the bookstore. Charlie was astounded by the number of Bibles to choose from. There were paperbacks, hardcovers, and leather-covered Bibles. As he read the introduction of the different Bibles, Charlie swayed from one foot to the other, which gave him an anxious appearance. Charlie named the Gallup Waddle movement when he recognized what he was doing.

He considered the price of each one and selected a black semi-hard cover paperback book. He returned to the tall gentleman and said, "Thanks again."

Satisfied with his selection, he proceeded to the checkout lane with his credit card in hand. "No need to put the book in a sack; I'll carry it."

Charlie showed the receipt to the greeter as he left. He was ready to unlock the El Camino when he heard, "Can you help me? I haven't eaten in two days. I see you have a Bible, so you must be a Christian. Please share your wealth so I can get a McDonald's hamburger."

Charlie was hesitant. He didn't like to be panhandled.

The man wore ragged jeans and a jacket that was too large for him, but his hands and face were washed clean. Charlie turned his back on the man, reached into his billfold, took out a five-dollar bill, and faced the man. "Here, get yourself a good meal."

## Chapter Two

## Creation and Emergence

## Day Two

The following day, Chile Charlie and Dolly sat in the conference room while they waited for the others to arrive. Finally, the other members came with a drink in their hands.

"Shall we continue?" Dolly asked.

*I hope we don't have to put up with the usual chitchat before discussing the topic we came here to learn about, Charlie thought.*

Pastor Smith initiated the meeting. "Several universal truths or beliefs are embedded in the stories continually taught about life from generation to generation. Anthropologists can determine the values honored or discarded by groups through their relics and oral stories. I wonder if modern technology, such as social media, has changed these traditional beliefs in the minds of younger Navajos."

Padre O'Roke offered, "Many older Navajos who attend my church are afraid that modern-day lifestyle conflicts with their traditional beliefs.

For example, the question of what happens after death is a fear that the older generation in my congregation has because they fear spirits. They didn't want to look upon or touch the dead body. The home of the dead had to be destroyed. However, the younger generation does not hold the fear of the departed spirit. They no longer think of destroying one's home."

"Interesting," Charlie added, "I did a research paper on death in diverse cultures during my undergraduate work. I was surprised about how other cultures described and handled death. Equally remarkable was the tendency for us to see contrasting features across cultures. We sometimes do not recognize the similarities we share."

Pastor Smith said," That's all well and good, Charlie, but you should recognize the influence of formal and informal education on one's culture.

Many times, these differences lie in the bailiwick of politics. Education and politics march together to fashion the culture. Politics provide governance, and education is the conduit to governance. An example of what I mean is when the government established schools for the Navajo children to learn and think white."

Painted Cloud spoke, "Many of these differences lie in the issue of who should be in control. Therefore, to maintain power, people are led to believe in bad mistakes or ideas in other cultures before experiencing them. For instance, some think Navajo tribe members only know poverty, waving, and getting drunk."

Painted Cloud twisted in his chair, and his face turned red with anger. He added," I recently read an opinion piece in *Beyond Today* by Scott Ashley, stating that is not what people believe, but I don't think that's true.

Cities, states, and countries can be divided by politics. We must study and learn the written and oral stories of the histories and traditions of cultures we do not know."

"Was Ashley right?" Charlie asked.

"I'm not sure, but I think he was. Political messages can be spun to set the stage, creating dislike or hatred, if you will. Let's not forget that the Navajos were once described as savages, and if you recall, some in the conservative media painted all Muslims as bad a few years back," Painted Cloud said.

"What is your definition of political myth?" Charlie asked.

Painted Cloud said, "My definition of political myth parallels Henry Tudor. In 1975, in his book *Political Myths,* he wrote that myths are believed to be true even with faults. They are devices with dramatic construction used to come to grips with reality. That's my definition. For example, someone else shot JFK other than Oswald, and Obama wasn't born in the United States."

Pastor Smith wanted the group to understand that politics and comparative methodologies are the same from his viewpoint. They both create a picture of humanity in the past, present, and future but did not voice that idea.

The room temperature was comfortable during the morning, but as the sun rose higher, Charlie wished that the air conditioner would start. A minute later, Charlie's wish came true. The room temperature again settled back to cozy seventy-two degrees.

▲▲▲▲▲

Charlie turned to Painted Cloud and asked a litany of questions: "Why does corn play such a vital role in the spiritual life of the Navajos? How does corn pollen work within a Navajo ritual? How essential is it? Why is it so prominent? Where does it say that corn pollen is omnipresent?"

Painted Cloud answered, "Navajo beliefs and rituals are multifaceted. Outsiders have trouble perceiving the foundation of corn in our culture. The inevitable question is: What are the sources of unity behind the diversity of the oral system? Let's see what evidence exists among the Navajo beliefs where there is contact with the divine."

"Why don't you start, Blue Rope?"

Blue Rope explained, "Corn and corn pollen are so repetitive in Navajo rituals that they go unnoticed. It is used in activities such as 'Blessing Way' and 'in-evil-ridding healing ceremonies."

Blue Rope continued, "Today, Navajos believe that corn, cornmeal, corn pollen, and the corn god operate against a background of the genetic Navajo Indian beliefs in most matters. It is not an exaggeration to say that the Navajo manifest as a thoughtfully corn-centered culture and, to that extent, most of a corn-centered religion. For the sake of brevity, we will not list the ritual ways the Navajos use cornmeal."

Charlie inquired, "How is it made?"

Painted Cloud answered, "The pollen of the corn is the substance dusted off the tassels of corn. After it is collected, it is blessed and used as the primary means of communicating by many Holy People. It is used in ceremonies as a blessing and offered in prayer. Corn pollen is a pillar of traditional Navajo culture."

Dolly said, "I read that corn is used in making many traditional dishes, including kneel-down bread, blue corn mush, dried, steamed corn, and roasted corn. Corn pollen is a sweet-tasting, yellow-colored powder collected from mature corn plants' tassels. Because corn, or maize, has traditionally been a life-giving staple of indigenous groups throughout the Americas, the pollen, which is necessary for corn's survival via pollination, has attained a sacred, life-giving status of its own. Often kept in small leather pouches, corn pollen is used in ceremonies as a blessing and offered in prayer."

Pastor Smith stood, pointing to the wall, and said, "This sand painting is not now, or is rarely, performed during the Navajo Blessing Way or Beauty Way ceremonies. Also, this sand painting is not of the Nine-Night Way.

"What is the Nine-Night Way," Charlie asked.

Padre O'Roke explained, "The Nine-Night Way is separate from the funeral itself. It's like the Irish wake and takes place nine days after the person's death. They celebrate their life at the point at which their spirit traditionally leaves the body."

▲▲▲▲▲

Painted Cloud submitted, "Here's how my elders explained this particular sand painting of a Corn Stalk to me."

As our spirit travels from another world, we travel on the Rainbow Path. Before you approach the Holy Grandfathers, you see four footprints that lead to the Holy Grandfathers who are there and who grant you renewal and reawakening. As you take the following four steps up the Corn Stalk, you're reborn into another world, making the next four steps as you experience the ugly and beautiful sides of life that help you to develop spiritually. The Corn

Stalk represents enduring the hardships of life and living a beautiful life—from birth into the transformation of old age.

That is where the Spirit Guides come into your life and instruct you on how you live your life, right or wrong. You're beginning to reflect on the spiritual processes to develop your spiritual capacity."

Blue Rope added, "The Rainbow Path consists of going on a spiritual journey, seen in the sand painting itself. It shows the rainbow with four footprints leading to the Holy Grandfathers. Then you start by going up the Corn Stalk, developing and relearning what we call — peace, beauty, balance, and harmony, experiencing your feminine essence, then the masculine essence, as you ascend the Corn Stalk. At the top of the Corn Stalk is the final stage of enlightenment, the result of being transformed by walking upon the pollen path. The bird at the top represents spiritual sovereignty."

Padre O'Roke added, "Like all other sand paintings, this 'Rainbow and Corn Pollen Path' is a visual prayer that tells us how to live on Mother Earth and throughout the many worlds—through time and eternity. So, this sand painting depicts the visual spiritual process of reaching the highest potential and capacity in one's spiritual development."

Painted Cloud concluded, "I'm sharing some of my Navajo spiritual knowledge and philosophy that reflects spiritual teachings through my life experiences of this Navajo ceremony and others. The Pollen Path symbolizes an individual's journey through life, and it is rich in myth and meaning. Created as a sand painting, it was used in ritualistic healing ceremonies during which community members gathered to support an individual on their spiritual exploits."

Blue Rope reached into his leather pouch and took out a small pinch of pollen. He turned to Charlie and Dolly with an on-stage flair and threw the pollen toward them, saying, "Bless you, and may you live in peace and harmony."

Now Blue Rope was silent. Charlie, in Navajo fashion, waited for a signal that Blue Rope was finished or collecting his thoughts.

"This description of the value of corn pollen was extremely enlightening. We learned so much about corn and corn pollen. Thank you," Dolly said.

Charlie nodded at Dolly and whispered, "It's time to get back to Gallup."

Dolly agreed. Charlie stood up and said, "Okay, gentlemen, we have gained important insights into Navajo Beliefs today. But Dolly and I need to get back to Gallup. We will return at nine in the morning."

▲▲▲▲▲

Dolly wet her lips, an old habit from her early days on the debate team said, "I found today's session had much more meat on the bones than yesterday, didn't you, Charlie?"

"That's right," Charlie opined.

"I am ready for dinner," Dolly said. "Let's find a diner for a giant hamburger, French fries, and a coke," Dolly offered.

'There you go, Dolly, reading my mind," Charlie said. "I'm so hungry I could eat two burgers," he grinned.

"Me too," Dolly repeated.

Fifteen minutes later, they pulled into the parking lot of Ben's World's Best Burger Joint.

They entered the oval glass front door that announced Ben's Place in Gothic gold lettering. The place was full of customers, and Charlie luckily spotted an empty booth. The stark, bright lights enhanced the cleanliness of the area.

Dolly and Chile Charlie sat side by side in a booth with a window so that he could keep an eye on the El Camino.

They placed their order for the hamburgers and the trimmings. While waiting for their meals, their cokes arrived. Dolly reached for her glass and took a long draw.

Drumming his fingers on the table, Charlie said, "The service has been excellent; I hope the food is good. I'm looking forward to filling my hungry belly."

Time passed slowly as they waited for their meal. Finally, two plates arrived with a giant hamburger on each plate. "Man, those burgers are huge; I'm not sure I can eat two. What do you think?"

"Yea, one will fill me up," Dolly said as she took a bite.

They started to eat like famished sailors but slowed down after three big bites.

"These are great burgers," Charlie stated.

## Chapter Three

## Myths and Legends

# Day Three

Chile Charlie and Dolly wanted to learn firsthand about the similarities and differences between the Bible and the Diné's Spiritual Beliefs, but the group had hardly touched on the subject.

Dolly initiated the meeting again. "When studying how humanity's roots and social aspects started, I found associated stories were traced back to other cultures. We can use the Bible's book of Genesis and the Navajo Emergence as a starting point. Is that all right with you all?"

"Let's not dilly-dally around all day," Charlie said with frustration.

Painted Cloud spoke slowly, "The Creation stories of the Navajo tribes contain similarities and differences to the Christian Bible's Creation stories. And if you compare these to the Christian stories, you will find several more differences unfold. As a Navajo Shaman, I must understand the implications of these similarities and differences in today's world for the Navajos I serve.

Therefore, the question we will attempt to answer is how the Creation stories of the Bible compared with the oral stories of the Navajo tribes."

"Good, now let's start," Charlie said anxiously.

Pastor Smith offered, "There is a difference between the Creation of the universe in the Bible and the Creation of the First Woman and Man in the Navajo beliefs. There is a reference to the culture in both stories to describe the world's beginning."

Dolly offered, "Yes, many versions must be analyzed to obtain the similarities and differences between the Western Bible writings and the Navajo Emergence stories. We can address language, story form, and the origin of these stories for the basis of our discussion."

Painted Cloud responded slowly but authoritatively, "Creation and Emergence are the same. The Navajo sometimes use Emergence as a word for Creation. The English language is too complex for me to understand. This is especially true when talking to my traditional Navajo tribe members."

"Scholars have separated the entire Genesis Creation of the earth first and then humans. For example, Genesis 1:1 – 31 states that God first created the heavens and the earth. The earth was without form and void, and darkness was over the face of the deep. And the Spirit of God was hovering over the face of the waters. But God said, 'let there be light, and there was light, and God saw that light was good. And God separated the light from the darkness. God called the light day, and the darkness he called night," Pastor Smith added.

Painted Cloud asked, "Then, did God call upon the orbits, planets, and stars to tell them to go to the 16 Whoop? as in the Navajos' beliefs."

Pastor Smith ignored Painted Cloud's question regarding the 16$^{th}$ Whoop. "Painted Cloud, your point of view was refreshing to hear. I want to say that God speaks of several aspects of the world, or earth, into existence throughout Genesis, and instead, it happens. For example, after God created the earth, he placed vegetation and trees on the land and fish and whales in the waters. Next, he created a man from dust and a woman from a man's rib. God did not think a man should live alone."

Painted Cloud inserted," But in the Navajo stories, the sun had the sole power to communicate, a significant difference from the Creation stories. One of the most striking is that a woman is made with a man in the Navajo version. They were made under the same buckskin simultaneously."

Dolly added to Painted Cloud's statement, "The first man and the first woman in the Navajo stories also had twins, but these twins were hermaphrodites. People would consider these stories of the Creation of humans a myth rather than a legend."

Charlie argued, "Still, the label 'myth' does not invalidate the story's impact on the Navajo culture. Several noteworthy features are applied to today's society, both on and off the reservation."

Padre O'Roke added, "For example, there is a myth regarding wolves. Many Navajo tribes consider wolves to be closely related to humans. This belief is because of the wolf's dedication to his pack, a trait the tribes attributed to themselves. The Navajo tribe was known for performing healing ceremonies where they could call upon wolves to restore the health of the ill."

Painted Cloud said, "Remember, evil and sickness are highly related in the Navajo culture. However, evil does not have the same connotation in the Navajo world. Balance is important. Good and evil are necessary for the Navajo society to function properly in Navajo eyes."

Pastor Smith had a point to make: "Genesis notes a similar sentence from God that says: 'God said it was good.' The main difference between these two stories is at the beginning of the Creation.

Painted Cloud added, "The Navajo stories talk about several creators of the earth. God notes only one, God as the creator of heaven and earth. There's no mention of heaven in the Navajo stories. However, there is a description of a space-like figure on these hoops that could be passed through. The creator breathed the elements of the earth to form it -- there was buckskin, two ears of corn, and the feather of a white eagle. The wind blew over the buckskin, ears of corn, and the feather of a white eagle. The ears of corn disappeared, and a man and a woman lay in the corn's place."

Pastor Smith gazed directly at Painted Cloud. "In the Bible, there was nothing initially except the spirit God and darkness and the face of the deep. You may not know the term deep, but it means the earth had no form. The Lord unilaterally created the universe out of nothing. The native stories and the Bible tell us that God made humans and animals after plants were put on the earth. In the story, God put humans on earth, which grieved the Lord's heart."

Charlie sensed condescension building within the group. "How about taking a fifteen-minute break to stretch, get a drink, and regroup."

When they returned, Charlie spoke first with a quote from Genesis 6:7 "The Lord says I will destroy man whom I have created from the face of the earth, both man and beast and the creeping things and fly in the air, for it saddens me that I have made them."

"I agree," Dolly said. "It is the planting of seeds on earth. The Navajo stories say that unknowingly, a God-like power planted the trees and covered the earth with green, but the Bible tells us in Genesis 1: 'That the earth brought forth grass and herbs yielding seed after its kind, and the trees yielding fruit, whose seed was in it. God liked it and approved. The purpose of humans was not only meant to eat the plants but to protect every little pebble alongside them."

With anger in his eyes, Painted Cloud responded, "The view of the value of earth and everything on it impacts the lifestyle of the Navajo tribes. They are widespread beliefs that everything has a spirit. This view contrasts with the selfish view of the Bible. It implies that humans deserve whatever they grow."

Dolly commented, "Genesis 2:7 reads, The Lord formed man from dust from the ground and breathed the breath of life into his nostrils, and man became a living creature." She was proud she had remembered the Scripture.

Pastor Smith gave her a wink and approving nod.

Painted Cloud added to the conversation, saying, "In the Navajo version of the sun, everything looks nice, and bursting is about to occur, but someone should be the caretaker of the people's land."

Charlie said, "But in Genesis 1:26 and 1:27, God says, 'Let us make man in our image, after our likeness: and let them have dominion over the fish of the sea, and the fowl of the air, cattle, and over all the earth, and every creeping thing that creepeth upon this earth. So, God created man in his image. He blessed them and told them to be fruitful, multiply, replenish the earth, and subdue it. God put humanity on earth to plant and harvest the bounty."

Dolly stood up and stretched. "When the Europeans began settling here, the Navajo tribes' hunting grounds were reduced. And as the settlers infiltrated the reservation, some of the European churches were built on the sacred grounds of the people. Many Navajo clans uphold traditional beliefs, including the Creation stories in their spiritual lives. Unfortunately, none of the stories are written, only passed down orally."

"Yes, that's true," Painted Cloud continued, "And I want to add that the Chuska Mountains were gifted with herbs and medicines for the first Woman and Man in the Navajo legend. From the time of Emergence, those mountains provided the same livelihood for the Navajo tribes, including protection from their enemies."

Pastor Smith added that the Navajo tribes have oral stories of their universe's Emergence. "However, today, Christianity heavily influences the Navajo nation. You can see that by the increasing number of Navajos who attend mass."

Continuing, he said, "According to the Bible, despite the differences between stories that make cultures what they are, the significant similarity is that people are given a second chance. Evil past actions can be forgiving because Jesus paid for the Sins of all humanity."

Painted Cloud reported, "Some clans use ceremonies to perpetuate their Spiritual Beliefs. Each clan may recognize different Emergent stories."

▲▲▲▲▲

Pastor Smith told the group he had to make an important phone call and asked for another short break. Soon after, they all returned to their seats.

"Padre O'Roke, please give us your take on how Christianity began to influence the Spiritual Beliefs of the Navajos," Charlie asked.

"Yes, of course, I will," he responded slowly and methodically. "According to archaeologists, Christianity began in Jerusalem in the first century during the Roman occupation. It then migrated throughout Europe and later across the ocean to North America. Many Europeans came from Romania and journeyed to the Americas in the early 1800s. They migrated to escape religious persecution, as did the Jews and Irish, to name a few. Christianity began to influence the Native Americans and especially the Navajos throughout America."

Charlie interrupted, "Padre, do you think the aggressive Europeans attempting to take the land and force Christianity beliefs onto the Navajos caused many problems?"

Padre cast his eyes up to see divine inspiration from heaven. "Historians who contribute to Wikipedia say 'yes.' You will find several interpretations when looking for similarities and differences between the Bible and the Navajo beliefs. The Navajo stories were passed down through traditional oral stories. At the same time, the Holy Bible has several interpretations due to the translations of changing languages worldwide, which changes the meaning of these stories.

Chile Charlie said, "In 2019, when I was taking a class on Navajo Beliefs at New Mexico University, I was told many Navajo stories were translated into English from the Navajo mother-child so we could read them. Some word meanings will forever be lost in translation."

."The Bible passages we now read are taken from the King James version," Pastor Smith said.

"The authors of the Navajo stories were tape-recorded and written down. Some storytellers include new aspects into the account based on their sacred dreams. They are deemed valid due to the importance of dreams of the Navajo culture, as a way their ancestors speak to them. And the forms from which these stories were taken could be different and disjointed. In the Bible, stories are written together, and the reader can see the linkage."

Dolly looked eager to say something, "Genesis 2:7 says that God formed man out of dust and breathed life into man. Similarly, Navajo stories tell that the sun created humans out of the glowing gases from the sun and a vein of a cedar tree molded by the wind. Both stories show that humankind was created from the earth. However, Navajo stories of the beginning of human beings are similar because they need elements from several powers. But it is different because the sun sheds a tear into the earth, forming a blood clot that is molded into a human.

"What about the woman? When were they created and by whom?" Charlie asked.

"The Bible story explains that God loved Adam and didn't want him to be alone. He carved out a rib, filled it, and called it woman," Painted Cloud answered. "But in the Navajo stories, the woman is created from a different rock-- the moon.

Padre O'Roke explained, "The element for the Navajo narration was from the sun, not God's wrath like in the Bible. But his teardrop was included. The final important detail regarding the Creation of humans is the Creation of women besides the man. In the Bible stories, women were made after men. Genesis 2:18 says man should not be alone. A woman should be a man's helper."

Painted Cloud stood behind his chair, turned around twice, sat down, and started again, "In my clan's beliefs, women were made differently. The sun called all the planets and supernatural together, and when they were assembled, the sun, in a bright flash, took out one of his eyes, and he threw it to the wind, and it became the moon. The story continues when this new orb, the eye planet, created the woman, a planet Virgin, and a moon maiden. She created other women in her shadow. She wanted them to walk on the earth."

Blue Rope proudly said, "In the Dine´ stories, the woman was created from the sun, not from a man's rib like in the Bible. In both stories, the first children of the first people are two boys. Their names were Cain and Abel in the Bible; however, their names are unknown in the Navajo legends, but they were twin brothers."

"The Bible says it took seven days to create humans. However, one day is with the Lord as one thousand years and the one thousand years as one day."

Pastor Smith mentioned, "That the entire world, with the first human being, took seven million eons in the Navajo stories."

"Holy cow, whoever thought time could pass so fast," Charlie explained. "Dolly and I must return to Gallup for the Navajo Art Museum Grand Opening. So, let's call it a day and continue our discussion tomorrow at nine o'clock."

# Chapter Four

## Myths and Legends Continued

## Day Four

Charlie and Dolly left Gallup later than they anticipated. Charlie had to drive faster than he wanted to reach their destination before the group assembled. Charlie and Dolly were excited about what would happen today. They wanted to arrive on time. The other group members were on mañana time. (A Spanish word meaning tomorrow often indicates an unspecified time.) At 9:15, everyone had their cups filled and ready to start the discussion.

Again, Painted Cloud started, "In the Navajo tales and the Bible, a Great Flood occurred. There are separate tales about the Emergence of the Navajo people, just as there is a separation of tales about the Great Flood destroying the earth. However, the Navajo stories do not explain the Great Flood, except that the great spirit may have been angry with the humans and let the water monster flood the earth because he wanted to make better humans."

Dolly added, "These floods wiped out most living things in Navajo and Christian stories."

"In the Bible, floods happen because of similar reasons. God saw how great man's wickedness was, and everything man conceived was evil," Pastor Smith said.

"In both stories, there are survivors," Painted Cloud added. "In the Diné's legend, one beautiful girl survives when the great Eagle flies down, grabs her with its talons, and flies her safely to the top of a high mountain. In the Bible, Noah and his family survived because God commanded him to build an arc."

"Because of the family dynamics of the survivors, it was implied in Genesis that Noah had three sons who began to populate the earth," Charlie interjected. "His children were divided into different nations. Likewise, there are tales where the girl and the eagle bear children. Both bestiality and incest are now considered taboo in most cultures."

"There has always been a close connection between people and animals in the Navajo culture," Painted Cloud said.

"Again, the woman in the story bore twins, one boy and one girl, like the Navajo's stories of the beginning. In the Navajo stories, the people could not stop committing adultery. Males were forced in that direction. This action gave them God-like powers to ignore their people.

"There are obvious parallels here with the Great Flood. There's another underlying parallel story of Adam and Eve being kicked out of the Garden of Eden for eating the forbidden fruit from the trees of knowledge of good and evil. God sent them out of the Garden."

Dolly put her hands together in the shape of a steeple. The group looked at her. She mentioned that she was ready to change the subject.

"What do you have to say, Dolly," Charlie asked.

Dolly explained, "Well, today, the Navajo tribes have a matriarchal society, and I wondered if that is because of their legend of female Emergence. The female was not from man but from the sun. The Navajo stories are a testament to the female being alongside with man. This belief affects the matriarchal system of the Dine´."

"I am ready to stretch, get some coffee, and give my mind a rest. How about a fifteen-minute break?" Charlie asked.

When the group reassembled, Charlie said, "Dolly is exhausted from the information exchange and would like to continue tomorrow, okay?"

There was agreement within the group, and everybody departed. Charlie and Dolly rode in silence.

*Charlie wondered if the Navajos' original myth had a basis of truth. And another word for Wolf in the Navajo language is a witch. The Navajo fear of wolves derived not from the animal but rather from the potential for monstrous behavior from humans. The Navajo believes that human witches use or abuse the wolf's power to influence others. Some Navajo tribesmen deliberately turn antisocial, away from nature's golden means of balance, and choose unnatural evil.*

Charlie formulated a plan to discover the answer to the question. He looked at Dolly momentarily before asking her, "Dolly, what are your thoughts about the value of Skinwalkers' stories in the Navajo spiritual world?"

Dolly didn't answer that question. She said," Charlie, it has been a long time Since we had lunch. Let's have dinner at the El Rancho Restaurant."

# Chapter Five

## Blue Rope

## Day Five

Charlie thought he needed to unpack yesterday's information. He wanted to have a face-to-face talk with Blue Rope. Waiting for the right moment, Charlie quietly approached the Shaman to join him for iced tea under a nearby tree. Blue Rope accepted.

They found an inconspicuous area with constantly chipping birds in the background and two comfortable wooden chairs in the shade. The afternoon sun was low in the sky, and there was not even a hint of wind. Charlie looked at the tree. The leaves didn't move. He felt strange for the stillness, which was calming after all the back-and-forth discussion indoors.

"Why'd you want to talk to me, Charlie? I said all I could say inside," Blue Rope asked.

Leaning back in his chair, Charlie asked his newfound friend to remove his head cover mask. Charlie wanted to dig deep into Blue Rope's emotions, and the mask was a hindrance.

Blue Rope hesitated, then took both hands and gently removed his mask. He shook his head to allow his long hair to find its natural place on each side of his head. His face was not a surprise. Blue Rope had deep-set brown eyes, a straight, defined nose, a smile with discolored teeth, and a square chin.

He settled back in his chair and smiled.

"Thanks, the mask was getting warm," Blue Rope whispered.

▲▲▲▲

Charlie smiled. Blue Rope had said little throughout most of their discussions. Charlie thought Blue Rope could help him find the answer about witchcraft in the Navajo culture.

*Charlie wondered if Blue Rope would disagree with his thesis about the superstitions of Wolves. He remembered that Blue Rope reported superstitions were simply a procedure giving people a necessary outlet for blame in times of trouble and frustration.*

"Wolves are admired for their superb hunting skills, and the Navajos are known for performing healing ceremonies where they would call upon wolves to restore good health to the ill," Blue Rope said.

"Navajos are big into nature. Every aspect of their lives is a ceremony of nature, including building a Hogan or planting crops. All ceremonies, including songs, prayers, and sand paintings, were used as a spiritual way to heal the sick," Blue Rope added.

Chile Charlie leaned back with his hands locked behind his head, "Blue Rope, do Skinwalkers' stories provide direction to the Spiritual Beliefs of the Navajos today?"

"The Navajo legend about Skinwalkers has mixed reviews. The concept of the Skinwalkers is not well understood outside our culture. This is due to reluctance to discuss the subject with outsiders not living or believing our experiences," Blue Rope stated.

"Please enlighten me," Charlie responded.

Blue Rope added, "The Skinwalker is an ancient Navajo legend that takes on various forms across our tribes. They are a wicked sorcerer who can transform, occupy, or disguise themselves as animals. The myth behind this change is relegated to simply too much peyote, a hoax, or oral traditions in the Navajo beliefs. We have always had a hodgepodge of cultures, folklore tales, and nasty critters of the deep.

Also, the Skinwalker stories told to young people usually are life and death struggles. Either the Skinwalker or the Navajo killing one or the other. Sometimes they encounter stories that end in a draw or the Navajo wins. Other times if the Skinwalkers are approaching a Hogan, they are scared away."

"Then again, stories may take place on a road where the child is vulnerable. But they escape in an untraditional way," Blue Rope said, stopping to take a long drink of his iced tea.

Charlie saw an opening to ask, "Were these stories part of the development of discipline among young people?"

Blue Rope said, "Yes, you could say that."

"Nevertheless, Navajo witches, including Skinwalkers, represent the antithesis of Navajo cultural values. While community healers and cultural workers, known as medicine men and women, use the stories to perform their so-called magic, traditional healers learn about both the good and evil values of the stories. Most can handle the responsibility, but some Skinwalkers can become corrupt and choose to become negative."

Charlie asked, "Has the concept of Skinwalkers ever been linked to the Navajo Emergence myths?"

Blue Rope continued. "Yes, they were once thought to be helpers of the Divine Beings. They were agents for the Holy People when they first trained humans in the Blessing Way."

"Therefore, Navajos are reluctant to reveal Skinwalker stories to those they do not trust. Fortunately, Charlie, I trust you with this information." Blue Rope said as he began to stand up.

He decided it would be better not to stand. Instead, Blue Rope twisted in his chair somewhat defensively and said, "The Navajo wolves are strictly psychotherapeutic and are considered harmless." He reached into his gourd container, pulled out an eggs-size turquoise stone formed like a frog, and tossed it to Charlie.

Then Blue Rope uttered, "This is a Reed Clan totem, good for fending off death. No self-respecting Navajo Wolf will bother you. I guarantee it.

Wolves are called upon to restore health from illnesses. Wolves were admired for their superb hunting skills, and prayers were often offered to honor them before warriors went on their running expeditions.

The Dine´ believes the fear of Wolves arrives not from the animal but rather from the potential of their devilish behavior. They thought that human witches used the Wolves' power to influence or abuse other humans. Wolves were used as tools to depict danger.

Navajos believe the Great Spirit will judge the soul's immortality at death by the good and evil deeds of the person."

Blue Rope stopped and pondered for a while. "Charlie, you brought in the word mortality. I must tell you that mortality and religious belief sometimes conflict. For example, Navajos believe that blood vengeance is a process many clans use to resolve animosity. As one Shaman said, blood is the foundation for the Navajo legal system."

*Chile Charlie was interested in a segment of the Navajo culture that put drums at the forefront. Charlie wanted to know the significance of the drum's size and which drums were used in which ceremonies.*

Charlie asked Blue Rope to tell him about the significance of drums in the Navajo culture.

Blue Rope answered Charlie's inquisitive thought saying, "In the Navajo culture, the drum is looked upon with great respect and dignity, representing the sacred heartbeat of Mother Earth. In Navajo circles, the drums play an important role in ceremonies, celebrations, and spiritual festivals. Through songs and dances to the drum beats, the Navajos try to find a close spiritual relationship with the creator, the mysterious powers they look to as gods. Because the Navajo culture has always believed in the circle of life, many believe that the drum beats in their ceremonies are the heartbeat of their Mother Earth."

Blue Rope added, "The drum beats heard in these ceremonies are produced by various drums. There are hand drums that are used many times in spiritual ceremonies where a lot of singing and dancing occur. There are drums made from animals like deer, elk, moose, and even buffalo. These drums are often played at tribal council and produce loud, booming drum beats. Water drums are just as they sound. They are drums that are partially filled with water.

The drum beats of water drums are distinctive, and their sound differs depending on the liquid in the drum and any physical activity.

During peyote ceremonies, they produced drum beats from various-sized instruments. Traditional Navajos say the drum beat can change natural elements, including the weather. It is believed to have the power to heal sickness; some think it can send messages to the animal and spirit worlds. We Navajos Americans look at the drum as a living and breathing entity; we believe that the spirits of the tree and animal that the drum are made from life within the drum. We think the drum beats help call out to these spirits to protect and watch over us."

With a sparkle in his eye, Charlie turned to Blue Rope, shook his hand, and gave him a nod. "Let's join the others?" Blue Rope and Charlie walked side-by-side as they rejoined the group. Charlie didn't ask another question as they returned to the conference room.

▲▲▲▲▲

Pastor Dan Smith, Padre Damon O'Roke, Painted Cloud, and Dolly returned to their chairs in a relaxed frame of mind.

"Did you two enjoy the iced tea and the comfort of the outdoors," Dolly asked.

"Yes, we did, yes, we did!" Charlie said.

The break was over. All members were in their seats. Charlie was delighted to start the session with the question about revenge.

"In the Old Testament, revenge was described as an eye for an eye and tooth for a tooth. However, the practices among Navajos were far more complicated than the Scripture portrays. The law of blood grounded in the structure of the Navajo society is not an act between the public but is a private matter between the clans of the victim's assailant," Painted Cloud interjected.

"Killing in a clan is a legal right and a duty to enforce legal revenge. Simultaneously, they have a sacred obligation to produce life in exchange for the original victim to be indifferent or unresponsive when the victim's family for revenge. Sometimes, the system did not work, and blood feuds developed between clans. However, for the most part, the retaliation killings returned conflicting clans to the state of balance, which many Navajos tried to acquire," Blue Rope stated.

"The revenge has spiritual significance, for some Navajos believe the deceased could not enter the spiritual world until his relatives had avenged the killer. Blood revenge thus allows a Navajo to channel the despair and hatred spine by the violent telling in a normal process with the effects of a potentially dangerous feud between clans," Padre O'Roke said.

Charlie stood up and stretched. "The issue of Navajo revenge will require more thought on my part, but what is the significance of the ghost dance?" Charlie asked.

"A late-nineteenth-century American Indian spiritual movement, the ghost dance began in Nevada in 1889. A Paiute named Wovoka (Jack Wilson) prophesied the extinction of white people and the return of the old-time life and superiority of the Indians," Dolly said.

"How was it performed," Charlie asked.

"It was a traditional circle dance with Singers and drummers who play a rhythmic song that allows the spirits to enter. The early purpose of the dance was to unite the living souls of the dead to help restrict American Western expansion. The believers hoped the movement would bring peace, prosperity, and unity to the Navajos and the other Native Americans," Painted Cloud explained.

"Despite the widespread acceptance of the ghost dance movement, Navajo leaders subscribe to the ghost dance as worthless words," Pastor Smith said.

"The Wounded Knee Massacre was not the end of the ghost dance. Instead, it went underground. The dance became a private ceremony," Dolly said.

Painted Cloud stated, "Modern writers believe the movement did not gain traction with the Navajos because the Navajos had a higher social and economic presence. Another factor was cultural norms among the Navajos, which taught the fear of ghosts and spirits based upon past practices."

Dolly said, "With all this critical information to process, I feel overwhelmed. I want to spend some time going over my notes. Would it be OK if we call it a day?

"We did not intend to overwhelm you, Dolly, but to fully understand the Navajo culture, you must know the facts and background we provided," Pastor Smith said.

"OK, that is it for today. We will see you again tomorrow at nine o'clock," Charlie said optimistically.

# Chapter Six

## Salvation and Sin

### Day Five

Before he spoke, Painted Cloud stood with hands extended for all to be quiet. He wanted all those present to pay close attention. He said, "Salvation is not a word used by the Navajo to discuss death afterlife. They believe in Chindi, the spirit that remains after the person dies. But that spirit does not embody every aspect of a person's soul. Instead, it consists of all the negative parts of that person."

Pastor Smith added, "To avoid becoming a Chindi victim usually, the byproduct of violence, Navajos must follow the rules of traditional beliefs. The Chindi is a spirit from Navajo beliefs and consists of everything terrible about the person who died. Failing to honor the burial of a person properly can also bring about a Chindi, as well as never mentioning the deceased's name. The Chindi is known to haunt houses for decades where the death occurred."

Painted Cloud added, "Navajos believe contact with this ghost can bring the victim a disease they call 'ghost sickness.' Navajos limit contact with the dead. They stay away from places where the person died. Navajos limit speaking about the dead."

Blue Rope said, "If someone becomes ill, the Chindi is blamed. Navajos gather at the haunted site and perform rituals to restore balance to the world of the living."

Padre O'Roke added, "In the traditional Navajo beliefs about death, a Chindi is not all that remains of a person's soul after death."

Painted Cloud said, "Navajos believe in the afterlife, but they traditionally do not believe it in the same way as Christians. Both Navajos and Christians believe the body needs to be cleaned. But similarities don't stop there. When someone dies in the Navajo culture, others traditionally cleanse the body.

Two or more men wearing only moccasins would cover the body with a coverlet. They enclose the naked body with ash to protect against evil spirits. Once the body is ready for burial, the body is put on a horse. Preferably, the horse would be one the dead person recently acquired. Once they find a suitable space, they kill the horse and bury it with the Navajo-prepared body. The belief is that the deceased would need the horse for the afterlife."

Blue Rope reported, "The Navajos don't always bury the dead. They sometimes hid them."

Painted Cloud stated, "Handling the body during the ritual is important. Navajos believe the dead person's Chindi would more likely haunt the living. Only the persons in the death and burial party look upon the body."

Charlie asked, "Do Navajos ever use coffins to bury the dead?"

Blue Rope offered, "Not often, but they leave the coffin slightly open when they do. This allows the spirit to escape to the afterlife."

♦♦♦♦♦

Pastor Smith said, "In Christianity, Salvation saves humans from Sin and its consequences. It includes death and separation from God. Deliverance or redemption can be a substitute word. Christ's death and resurrection are the justifications for Christian's Salvation."

"Sin separates us from God and incurs his wrath, but anyone who makes peace with Him shouldn't fear death. If you're saved, don't fear Satan's clutches. A relationship with Jesus gives you the path to everlasting life! If we turn from Sin and follow Jesus, we can rest easy! Heaven is waiting for all those who die," Padre O'Roke told the group.

"In scripture, Ephesians 2:5 tells us Salvation is God's gracious, deserved gift. And Acts 4:12 says the only path is through faith in Jesus Christ. We receive Salvation through faith, first by hearing the gospel. The next step is when we decide to believe and trust the Lord Jesus. We continue the relationship with God in heaven," Pastor Dan Smith added.

Dolly said, "But Salvation is only for those who know Jesus. Our mission is to spread God's Word to all who will hear. Remember, God sent Jesus, in the form of a man, to remove the Sin which separates humanity's heart from the heart of God. "

Pastor Smith said, "Jesus took the world's Sins and paid the penalty. Jesus cried while dying on the cross, "My God, My God, why have you forsaken me?"

Charlie bowed his head and said, "Christians believe that when God gave his son, He restored our opportunity for all mankind to be with God."

▲▲▲▲▲

"But what does the Bible say," Charlie asked.

"Sin is the transgression of the law. It is not violating one's conscience; it's breaking God's Law." Padre O'Roke said.

"Where did God's law come from?" Charlie asked.

Pastor Smith said, "God's law came from his character. God's law codifies how he thinks and acts. It is the will of the being who exists before the universe and humanity. And the Creator's will to love.

Every particle of human suffering, unhappiness, misery, and death has come solely from its transgression!

If you fulfill the holy law according to the scripture, 'thou shalt love thy neighbor as thy self,' you do well. The holy law explains the principle of love.

Love is the fulfillment of the law. Jesus fulfilled it, setting us an example that we should fulfill the law. We meet it with love--not any love we have by nature, but the love of God shared abroad in our hearts by the Holy Spirit. The Holy Spirit in God's law is in our lives."

Padre O'Roke continued, "So, if we fulfill this law, we do well--, but if not, we Sin. Verse 10-11 states that if we keep the whole law, the general principle of love towards our neighbor, yet, offers one point, we are guilty of breaking the holy law. Notice the points of law in James' description do not commit adultery or not kill part of the Ten Commandments.

Jesus Christ was the ultimate example of perfect obedience to the holy law. Most Christians believe that Christ came to earth to teach the Ten Commandments. He clearly stated, think not that I come to destroy the holy law or to profit; I come to fulfill it.

Jesus magnified the holy law and made it honorable. When we put a spiritual magnifying glass on the Ten Commandments, it is enlarged in spirit and principle into many more points. And the larger view of the entire Bible magnifies God's law. The law is the basis of all scripture. It defines God's way of life as happiness, joy, and eternal life. Genuinely fulfilling the Ten Commandments requires keeping both the letter and the spirit of the law."

Padre O'Roke gave two examples to illustrate this point.

"First, you heard it said in old times, thou shall not kill, and whosoever does is in danger of the bad judgment. Now, I say unto you that whatsoever is angry with his brother without a cause shall be in danger of a wrongful decision. He affirms that maliciously ending a human life is a Sin. Then he magnifies that law showing that the spirit of murder, which includes hatred, is also a Sin."

"Second: Christ addressed the seventh commandment, saying, " Ye have heard that it was said thou shalt not commit adultery. It tells us who should ever look at a woman with lust who has committed adultery with her already in his heart. Christ upheld God's law forbidding adultery, including premarital sex and infidelity within a marriage."

Pastor Smith said, "These examples show that Sin against God's law began in the mind and must be stopped immediately."

Sin is anything other than God's outflowing law of love. At the root of all Sin is vanity---loving self more than loving God or fellow man. It is manifested in attitudes of self-centeredness, self-exhalation, desire to be beautiful, covetousness, desire to get and take, jealousy and envy, competition, resulting violence and war, resentment, and rebellion against authority. These are the principles of spiritual Sin.

To repent of Sin means to quit Sinning and keep God's commandments, for if you break only one, you incur the penalty of Eternal death."

Chile Charlie said, "Thankfully, the sacrifice of Jesus Christ paid that penalty for us. Once someone repents, they are no longer doomed to eternal death. However, God still expects those he forgives to keep the Ten Commandments. What shall we say, then? Shall we continue in Sin, that grace may abound? God forbids, how shall we who are dead of Sin live no longer therein? Our responsibility is to overcome Sin—to choose not death but life."

Dolly Sweet Thompson said, "In 1 Timothy 6:10, 'For the love of money is the root of all evil: which while some coveted after, they have erred from the faith and pierced themselves through with many sorrows. And in Matthew 10:37, ' He that loveth father and mother more than me is not worthy of me: and that loveth son and daughter more than me is not worthy of me." These are two

Bible concepts that focus on evil. What are the Navajo beliefs regarding these matters?"

Painted Cloud offered, "The Navajo believes in good and evil, but that evil could take over if the universe were not in harmony. Ceremonies are held to honor the 'holy people' of Navajo culture. Navajo spiritual practice is about restoring balance and harmony to a person's life to produce health and is based on the ideas of Hózhóójí. The Diné believed in two classes of people: Earth People and Holy People.

Dolly asked, "What is *Hózhóójí*?"

Painted Cloud answered, "It has been said that *Hózhóójí* may be the most important word in the Navajo language. Often translated as 'balance and beauty,' the concept of *Hózhóójí* carries with it an essential emphasis on the state of harmony. It is the Navajo people's complex wellness philosophy and belief system. The principles guide thoughts, actions, behaviors, and speech. *Hózhóójí* is a means to improve a whole person's well-being and resilience.

Dolly said, "That is way over my head. Give it to me in plain English."

"It all boils down to maintaining a balance in life, never too extreme, either good or evil," Painted Cloud uttered and sat down.

When Dolly and Charlie begin to speak simultaneously, Charlie points to Dolly to go first.

"Thank you all for the most informative five days. To complete my dissertation. I have enough first-hand information about the Navajo oral stories that are similar and different from the Bible stories."

Dolly turned to Charlie. "Your turn."

"My deepest gratitude goes to Blue Rope for clarifying Skinwalker's myth. We will continue our new friendship long into the future," Charlie said.

There was a group hug, then Dolly and Charlie departed.

## Chile Charlie and Dolly's Recap

It was late afternoon when the meeting ended. The sun started dipping below the horizon, and its warmth evaporated. Dolly tucked her sweater close to her body as she stepped outdoors.

Charlie and Dolly were exhausted from the in-depth discussion of the final day. They are ready to return to Gallup. They said their goodbyes and thanked everyone for their hospitality.

Charlie opened the passenger door for Dolly, and she wiped the dust off the seat. They said goodbye to Tohatchi and the Chuska Mountains.

"Well, Dolly, give me your take on the past five days," Charlie questioned.

"The short answer is that the Navajos came to North and South America because of the dispersion at the Tower of Babel. Yet, connecting the migration dots requires more diligent research." Dolly said.

"I made a mistake when I didn't explore the comparison Turtle Back myth with the Book of

Genesis to determine if they were based on the same values," Dolly added.

Charlie stopped her and asked, "What in the world is the Turtle Back myth."

Dolly answered, "In the Navajo Emergence stories, many thought the Earth was created as the soil is piled on the back of a great sea turtle that continues to grow until it carries the entire world.

In the myth, the world's Creation begins with a great ocean, and far above was a Sky World where people like God lived. There were birds, a void of air, nothingness, and darkness.

This concept is like in Genesis, where the earth was in darkness and emptiness. As the culture of the Navajos evolved, so did the Creation stories. The gods created the ocean and all the creatures that lived in the sea and the sky.

In later accounts, the Navajo woman fell from the sky and became the Earth's creator and all land features. But in Genesis, there was only one Creator, and He created everything."

Charlie added, "In the Navajo myth, there was a married couple and a sacred tree at the center of the universe. The woman decides she wants some bark from one tree root, and her husband knows her desires could cause a problem but gives in to her wish. The husband took roots from the tree, dug a hole, and buried some of its origins. But the ground was not sick, and a hole was created. Filled was curiosity, the wife investigated the hole, and she tumbled into the hole. Their gods did not save her since she had disobeyed."

"There is a similarity between disobedience and punishment in Adam and Eve's story. They disobeyed God, eating the forbidden fruit of the tree in the Garden of Eden. They were banished from the perfect world God had created for them," Charlie concluded.

"Yes, all that is important. You know everyone needs faith. Whether it is religion, science, or the power of the universe, faith guides us. We must have faith in people. Everything is relative, even faith," Dolly stated.

There was a moment of silence between the two. Dolly leaned back on the headrest and went into a dream world. Her thoughts vacillated from the discussion of the past five days, the comparison between the Western Bible and the Navajo people's Spiritual Beliefs, and what kind of cowboy Chile Charlie was in bed.

Darkness encompassed the parking lot as they arrived at the El Rancho Hotel. They reached for their belongings and walked to the hotel holding hands.

"Charlie, thanks for all your help. I now must return to Chicago and put the last chapters of my dissertation to bed so that I can graduate this winter," Dolly said.

## THE END